# <u>Horace Rising</u>

**The Horace Chronicles #1**

*For all of those who never made it home, and for all of us who are still struggling to return.*

ISBN 978-0-9885801-5-2

# Table of Contents

# Chapter I:  The Deepest Scars of War

## *"Only the dead have seen the end of war."* ~ Plato

The staccato beat of the rotor-wash of the helicopter was getting louder.  The tempo of the waves increased.  And Horace was struggling to breathe as wave after wave crashed into his face more frequently.  He realized the Coast Guard helo was approaching at low altitude.  They had probably spotted him.  Taking a big gulp of air, he allowed himself to sink below the surface and used both hands to untie the shirt from his belt loop.  Resurfacing he waved it with his left arm over his head a few times while trying to keep himself on the surface with his right arm.  Then he tossed it high into the air and downwind, hoping it would unfold some and spread out on the surface.  It was the best he could manage for a distress signal.  Then he rolled onto his stomach into a Deadman's Float.  His entire left leg still convulsing and distorted with cramps, his fate was in the hands of the Coast Guard now.

"He's floating, LT.  He tossed something.  Looks like a shirt or towel," explained Petty Officer Jensen.

"What color, Chris?" asked the Lieutenant, hoping for some sort of confirmation that it was Chief MacDonald below her helicopter in the water.

"Blue.  Light blue, LT," replied the voice of her Crew Chief.

"Go!  Go!  Go!" shouted the pilot into her headset.  Horace was wearing a light blue fisherman's shirt when he jumped over the side of the boat.

"We're lowering the basket now," replied the Crew Chief.

"Roger that.  I'll hold her steady," the Lieutenant answered.

"Basket's away," the young man in the side door of the helicopter said matter-of-factly.

Sherrie Biggers worked the control to keep the big helicopter steady, thirty-five feet above the water below. Simultaneously, she scanned the horizon in front of her and the scene of destruction on the water, just hundreds of meters away. There was little left on the surface of Captain Hal's skiff. An explosion ripped it in two just a couple of minutes after she buzzed the gunman in the water. She radioed back in to Fort Myers, telling Commander Johnson that he could ground her later, but right now she was staying on station to search for survivors and render aid. He wasn't happy! Oh well. She'd deal with that later. Disobeying orders was still serious business, even in the Coast Guard.

"Diver ready," the Chief's tone carried a question mark.

"Deploy diver, Chief," said the Lieutenant.

"Diver in the water!"

Chris Jensen had been sitting on the edge of the deck in the side door of the big orange and white helicopter, the familiar vibration of the engines and rotors transmitting through her hips and legs and up her spine. You can feel it on the top of your head and out to your fingertips. The Chief rapped twice sharply on her helmet and Chris pushed free of the helicopter with her arms, falling into the frothing sea some thirty-five feet below.

The water felt warm and refreshing. Like a cork, she bobbed to the surface and turned in the direction of her target. Kicking strongly, she thrust one arm out ahead and began to swim.

Horace felt the water displacement of a diver entering the water in close proximity and heard the tell-tale whoosh of a large object slicing through the surface at high speed. Pushing both arms down and bringing them together, he raised his head. He grabbed a quick breath of air when his face found sunshine and tried to catch a glimpse of what was going on in front of him. Whirling shadow and light was all he saw before a wave took his head again. The rotor-wash of the chopper drowned out virtually all other sound.

A slender arm snaked around his chest under his arm from behind, crossing his collar-bone on the opposite side and squeezed tight. He felt the diver's body press firmly into his back. The Coast Guard Rescue Swimmer rolled him onto his back, head above water, and he was staring straight up at the flickering blades of the helicopter. There was spray and waves everywhere. It was hard to breathe without taking in water. He could tell the Rescue Swimmer was small, but strong. He relaxed and let the guy do his job, trying to keep his bad leg from convulsing again and mucking things up. Within seconds, something hard bumped into his head. A padded bar – the rescue basket! Horace flipped over and reached both arms forward to where he thought the basket should be. Finding purchase, he raised himself slightly with his arms and gasped for air. The diver scooped his legs and tossed him deftly into the floating litter. For the first time, Horace caught sight of the helmet and goggle clad rescue swimmer. The short sleeves of her neoprene wetsuit revealed smooth, tan, slender arms working deftly to secure a safety harness.

"He's a she," Horace thought, "I'll be damned."

Petty Officer Jensen climbed on board the basket, crouching over Horace's prone body. She snapped her own safety line onto the rigging and yanked hard on the main line from the helicopter's winch – twice. Then she motioned a thumbs up three times before grabbing on to the side rails of the basket. His leg convulsed uncontrollably, kneeing the Rescue Swimmer in the crotch. Letting out a quick breath, Chris screamed, "Hold still!" and dropped the full weight of her legs across Horace's to keep him from moving. He felt the line stiffen and the basket began to rise from the surface of the water. All he wanted to do today was try and catch a fish. Instead, he had been humiliated, shot at, and nearly drowned. How he was being rescued by a little girl.

"You're like a bad penny, asshole," he thought to himself as the winch on board the Coast Guard chopper pulled the basket into boarding position.

---

The white-hot bullets tore through his troubled sleep and tossed him fully conscious, gasping for breath, into the cold blackness of the night. Horace struggled to orient himself – to discover where he was, assess the threats, and check himself for damage. As the panic quickly turned to anger, then began to fade into frustration, he realized that he was in the familiar surroundings of the bedroom of his small apartment. He wasn't injured. He was laying in bed wearing a pair of boxer shorts. He was soaked in cold sweat and his mouth was so dry it felt like cotton. For a split second, he thought he could smell the familiar scent of mingled diesel fuel, cordite, and adrenaline over the stench of rotting garbage and human despair that were the hallmark smells of what had become his "other home" these past ten years. The sound of hot brass shell casings ejected from automatic weapons falling on to the broken concrete echoed into oblivion at the edge of his consciousness. Sitting up, he closed his eyes hard and shook his head to clear away the last vestiges of the nightmare that had interrupted his slumber.

Horace's eyes were still not quite focused, but they were tuned to the darkness. Looking at his dresser, he could see the clock. But he couldn't tell what time it was. "Damn these sleeping pills," he thought to himself. The meds that the doctors at the VA gave him to help him sleep better seemed to cause his blurry vision and made it difficult for him to focus for the first couple of minutes after waking up.

Sleep is precious to a guy like Horace. It becomes a choice between side-effects you can live with and problems you can't. It's a balancing act. And everyone has to find their own pathway to sanity. For Horace, the blurry vision is a serious problem, but one he is trying to manage. If he were still active there is no way he would tolerate blurred vision – not even for a minute upon waking. That could get him or someone on his team killed. But back home in the States and now out of the Navy, he tries to let it go. Sleep is worth the minute or two of diminished capacity to respond to a threat…or is it? Hell, his whole life had been about taking calculated risks! Now, in a strangely ironic twist of fate, he was taking this one trying to do what the experts call "make a successful transition from warrior to civilian." Bullshit! What experts? Who comes up with this crap anyway? These so-called "experts" never seem to have names. But just like hundreds of thousands of other combat veterans today, Horace has a name and his "transition" isn't something you can reduce to a 5 by 8" brochure or yet another Power Point Presentation. The meds might help him sleep better, which helped cut his anxiety and stress. But waking up almost blind tends to peg your stress meter when you've spent the past decade in Hell fighting enemies that appear out of nowhere, attack, and then disappear again just as quickly. When more of your teammates have been killed by the so-called "allies" you were there to help while they were eating, doing paperwork, sitting in meetings, just walking across a FOB, or even…yep…sleeping than during firefights or by IED's, waking up with blurred vision has a way of making you feel like a naked man caught in a crossfire – and that doesn't help!

Experience had been a cruel teacher. Horace knew that if he laid his head back down the nightmare would likely resume again, probably with a vengeance.

"Shit," he muttered as he swung his legs over the left side of the bed.

The constant dull pain in his left knee and thigh reminded him of the reason he was here.

"Good morning, Horace, you broken down war-horse," the reminder traveled from his repaired left leg to his brain so fast that no amount of Cognitive Therapy could stop it.

More "experts" had spent countless billable hours trying to teach Horace Hall sorts of nifty psychological tricks to intercept and re-program these negative thoughts into positive and less emotionally damaging thought processes, but that didn't diminish their omnipresence. The only things that could do that were contained in bottles – liquor bottles, pill bottles, or bottles of stuff that would kill him. For Horace, the bottled solutions to avoiding these unpleasant thoughts were not acceptable. The price tag was too high. In order to stop the thoughts he wanted to make go away, he had to consume enough liquor or psych meds to turn himself into a worthless alcoholic or a slobbering zombie. And suicide was off the table, the basest violation of the warrior code by which he lived. Suicide was the ultimate way to quit, admit defeat, to surrender. It left collateral damage and a mess for someone else to clean up. A warrior could never seriously consider suicide as a way out of anything. A warrior has only two options: to win or to go down swinging! So Horace was learning to live with the reality that he wasn't invincible, he wasn't even as good as he once was and never would be again, and with that damned blurry vision.

Whether it was two a.m. or just before dawn didn't really matter. Trying to sleep again now would just mean more nightmares. Flexing his muscles and wiggling his fingers and toes, Horace tried to get fresh blood coursing into his arms and legs to help ease the pain and clear his head. As he sat up on the edge of his bed, he paused to take a couple of deep breaths, shrug and rotate his shoulders, twist his torso to each side, and repeatedly flexed the muscles in his legs. In the months since his last surgery, this routine had become habitual. He no longer had to remind himself to do it before trying to stand up. Of course, after about the seventh or eighth time he fell down between his bed and the head, his keen instinct for self-preservation began to kick in. An embarrassing bruise and small gash over his right eye that lasted for a couple of weeks helped to remind him to warm up the motor before he tried to go anywhere. The corner of a bathroom counter top is very unforgiving at three o-clock in the morning.

At the VA clinic that same week his doctor had asked him if he had gotten into a fight, or if he had been drinking when he fell and hit his head. You would think these docs would know about the side-effects of the medications they put their patients on, but Horace had come to appreciate the difference between being able to rattle off a list of symptoms or side-effects and understanding that cuts, bruises, and the occasional trip to the emergency room were the most likely outcomes of "causes dizziness, blurred vision, and vertigo." Somehow, even these highly trained professionals failed to make that connection.

He liked his doc at the VA, a young fellow only out of medical school for a year or two who was no doubt paying back his enormous student loan debt faster by working for the government. The kid tried his best and truly cared about his patients. That's Hall Horace asked of anyone: give a damn and give your best. Everyone screws up. Nobody knows everything we wish we knew. This young doctor was always very respectful towards the veterans at the VA clinic and seemed to have a pretty good head on his shoulders about things – even things they don't teach you in college or medical school. So he got high marks from Horace.

"Alright, let's get this show on the road," Horace grumbled into the darkness. He still couldn't make out the hands on the clock well enough to tell what time it was.

"Dammit." And he rubbed at his eyes just before standing up.

Horace closed his eyes and fumbled for the light switch. The sudden change from darkness to artificial light would set his vision back a good five minutes if he didn't close his eyes before turning on the lights and then open them slowly facing away from the light source. Even this way, it took about fifteen seconds for his vision to stabilize.

The clock on the dresser read 5:32 a.m. Another day begins with a jagged edge. Could have been worse – a lot worse. Maybe today would be a good day.

"Let's see if we can get in and out of the head without tearing anything up, Chief," he said to himself under his breath as he shuffled into the bathroom. For better or worse, he was up for the day now. So he might as well make the most of it. And he had something in mind that just might put today in the win column.

---

After a quick shower, a dry shave, and couple cups of the nectar of the gods re-heated in a small microwave in the tiny kitchen of Horace's one bedroom apartment, he swiped his keys off the table and headed out the door into the dawn's early light. The familiar weight of his MILSPEC smart phone and a Leatherman multi-tool on one side and a Glock 26 on the other balanced out the main pockets of his Columbia breathable foul-weather shell as he climbed into his old Scout II 4x4. The morning dew was thick on the glass of the old truck he nicknamed "Kit" in honor of his boyhood hero, Kit Carson, the legendary scout for the U.S. Army from the western frontier of the nineteenth century.

Kit was one of the few possessions Horace had an emotional attachment to. But he had to admit that he was sort of fond of this beat up old example of the days when Americans built things that did what they were intended to do better, cheaper, and longer than almost anyone else in the world. Horace wasn't even in high school when Kit rolled off the production line in 1979, and here she was 33 years later – easier to get started in the morning than he was. The engine cranked on the first try and the aftermarket stereo system Horace had installed began belting out the lyrics and blues guitar licks from a ZZ Top tune on his iPod.

*Well I was movin' down the road in my V-8 Ford,*
*I had a shine on my boots, I had my sideburns*
*lowered.*
*With my New York brim and my gold tooth displayed,*
*Nobody give me trouble cause they know I got it*
*made.*
*I'm bad, I'm nationwide...*

Horace lit a Camel with the SEAL Team 1 Zippo he kept in the Scout and cracked the window. Then he hit the wipers and turned on the headlights and fog lamps. Still in the habit of always backing in to parking spaces, he was good to go with just the windshield and side glass cleared up enough to see. The friction of the air moving over the glass as he drove down the street would clear everything up in a few blocks.

Clearing the parking lot in front of the pay-by-the-week apartments where Horace was living, he turned left on to a wide paved county rod that ran along the Gulf of Mexico. Businesses along this stretch were sparse nowadays, but there were a few. Within a couple of miles in either direction he could get anything he needed or wanted, but near the old fisherman's camp turned motel and apartment complex where he lived right now there wasn't much more than a few bars, a pizza parlor, a pool hall, and convenience store spread over both sides of the road for a mile or so. It was quiet and he liked it that way.

Places like this folks now one another. When strangers like Horace show up, everyone notices. The neighbors sort of stick together and look after one another. If you're not here to cause trouble, they figure that out pretty soon because this is a tourist town. They survive on the money of strangers. And since the real estate collapse of 2008 and the BP Deep Horizon disaster in the Gulf, there isn't as much of it flowing around these days. So these small secondary communities along Florida's Gulf Coast are pretty hospitable and friendly places to anyone who shows up willing to pay for a room, meals, and the usual goods and services. Whether you're here to retire or just on vacation, that's how they make their living. They're pretty easy to get along with. It's the vacationers and some of the retirees from the North you have to watch out for.

Horace turned in to a well lit gas station and convenience store a few miles south of his apartment. There were several trucks pulling flats boats or bay boats sitting at the gas pumps and people were coming and going in and out of the store. It was the one place around for miles that was already buzzing with energy this early in the morning. He spotted the sky blue Action Craft he was hoping to see in the parking lot and backed Kit into an empty spot, hopped out, locked her up, and went inside.

Captain Hal was a big man with a bright smile and penetrating eyes. Built like an NFL linebacker late in his career, you would never guess the man to be in his mid-sixties. Horace had never seen him in long pants, and the man had calf and arm muscles that would make most of his teammates back in the SEALs jealous. But Captain Hal was fishing guide. That wasn't a military rank. Horace spotted him getting coffee and a breakfast sandwich, which meant he probably didn't have clients this morning. So far, things were progressing according to plan.

"Mornin' Captain Hal."

"Good morning, Horace! What are you doing out this early?" the big fishing guide asked.

Oddly enough, Captain Hal never smiled or joked around in here. He moved with purpose and had a serious look on his face whenever Horace had either bumped in to him here or come in here with him when they were fishing together. It was strange because the Captain was generally mostly jokes and smiles and even tended to spontaneously break out into song or whistle a tune – except for two times. Captain Hal turned to a man on a mission when his rig hit this parking lot and whenever he spotted a fish for someone on his boat. Then…suddenly…it was "game time," baby! And Captain Hal turned serious as any SEAL during an op Horace had ever worked with. It was one of the first things about the man that earned Horace's respect. He had what SEALs called, "the switch." But Horace couldn't figure out why he always flipped the switch here – at the gas station. Maybe it was just a ritual.

"I thought I'd roll the dice and run down here this morning and see whether or not you had paying customers today," Horace admitted.

"Looking for a freebie, are you? You know I don't do freebies," the charter captain stared Horace straight in the eyes with that hard-faced "man on a mission" look he reserved for the gas station.

"Oh no, sir. I pay my own way. I respect a man's right and need to earn a living and you're well worth your wages, Captain Hal. I'll gladly pay you. I was just hoping I might catch you here on your way out to fish without clients – sort of a spur of the moment thing. No offense," explained Horace.

"Well, I only have a half day to fish today. If that's okay with you then I'd be happy to take you out. You're damned fine angler and I always enjoy having you on the boat. You catch everything I point you towards. But you know my rate," and the captain suddenly handed Horace the breakfast sandwich and coffee he had been holding.

"Here, these are yours. I need to put some gas in the boat."

With that, the big fishing guide turned around and walked to the cash register where he paid cash for Horace's sandwich and coffee, some gas, a bag of ice for the cooler, and another cup of coffee for himself.

"Bring me a cup of coffee, will ya? It's already paid for," Captain Hal called across the busy convenience store.

"Coffee, Aye, Captain!" Horace replied. And the big man plunged out the front door, which clanged and jingled in his wake.

Outside, Captain Hal had already pulled the boat up to the gas pump and was topping off his tank by the time Horace got to his truck. He sat the coffees and biscuit sandwich on Kit's warm hood and reached into the back to retrieve a pair of St. Croix Legend Elite fly rods and his SmithFly boat bag. Inside the bag was everything else he would need, including a couple of Cheeky fly reels spooled up with different kinds

12

of Royal Wulff Bermuda Triangle fly lines and a couple of boxes of flies. He transferred the Glock and one extra magazine into the main compartment of the tackle bag and reached up onto the dashboard of the Scout and grabbed his Costa del Mar polarized sunglasses. Then he patted his pockets and double-checked each item to be sure he had everything before locking up Kit again. She'd be safe here. The guides coming out of The Rotunda often met some of their regular clients here. There were always a few cars parked here for the day. And there were always a few regulars sitting outside and wandering around. This place was a major gathering spot, unlikely as it may seem to an outsider. Vandalism was unheard of on this property. Horace quickly scooped up the coffees and stuffed the sandwich in his jacket pocket and headed for Captain Hal's rig.

"We're burning daylight!" said the guide as Horace approached the boat and truck with his arms full. He couldn't help but crack a smile. There was that serious look again.

Captain Hal told him to stow his gear in the boat.

"We'll rig up on the water. Give me that coffee. Thanks. Don't spill that in my truck!" said the captain as he walked around to the driver's side door.

"I'm not going to spill coffee in your truck…and I didn't even want the sandwich, but thanks. I won't eat it until we're underway," said Horace.

With that, the two men were off like a shot and headed for the public boat ramp just down the road at the end of the causeway that runs between Placida and Boca Grande. Inside the truck, Captain Hal began to sing.

---

On the water, the now jovial and relaxed guide eased the Action Craft boat out into Gasparilla Sound, looked around, and cut the motor.

"Let's rig up. What did you bring?"

"I've got a ten with an intermediate line and an eight weight with a floating line, and plenty of my own flies for trout, reds, snook, and light tarpon," Horace answered.

"Good. Rig that ten weight for tarpon. We're going up the river for juveniles first. Then we'll hit the flats and find some reds or snook. Sound like a plan?" Now Captain Hal was possessed of the familiar boyish excitement of a kid going fishing with his dad that Horace found so refreshing.

"You bet!" said Horace with a smile. And the two men sat on the water in the early morning sunrise rigging up fly rods and tying on leaders and flies for about fifteen minutes. Seagulls and pelicans cruised nearby and called out their morning greetings under a hazy late summer sky already thick with humidity. Horace wondered if they were talking to him or each other. He loved being on the water as nature awoke to a new day. It breathed life and hope into his weary soul. He paused for a few seconds and wished there was some magical way that these brief moments could be stretched out forever. Then he thought to himself: if there is a Heaven, it must be something like that – your favorite moments of peace, tranquility, and hope frozen for eternity. That would be awesome.

"You ready to go? We have fish to catch and they're not going to wait for us!" Captain Hal's voice interrupted Horace's philosophical introspection.

"Yessir. Let's blow this popsicle stand!"

---

Riding in the boat as it sped across the flats and protected bays reminded Horace of the countless hours he spent with the SEALs on small boats of many types and configurations. The wind on his face and smell of the salty spray, the gentle bumping over the light chop of the water's surface, and the hum and vibration of the boat's motor were all just as familiar to his senses as the bed you slept in at your parent's house when you were a kid. Absent were the tension of danger, the faint smell of military hardware, and the brotherhood. Those things were gone forever. In many ways, Horace was glad that part of his life was behind him now, but there seemed to be a hole in the middle of his soul that he just couldn't fill – the same way he felt when his parents had died in a car accident when he was fresh out of BUDS. And the same way he felt for a year and a half after his best friend in the teams, Mark Rizzolo, was killed in action in Iraq while Horace was back in the states attending some training that JSOC thought was more important than him being with teammates down range.

Horace had lost teammates before Mark died. He had even lost friends in battle. None of them effected him the way Mark's death had. SEALs knew that SEALs would die. You honored their passing and got back into the fight. That's the way they would have wanted you to carry on. That's how you honor a SEAL's memory. Eventually, Horace realized that the reason he was having so much trouble getting over Mark's death was that he wasn't there when it happened. For some reason, it was easier to let them go when you were there – when you knew that you had done Hall you could have done and that they went out swinging like the true warrior that they were. For a SEAL to die honorably in battle was not a bad thing. It sure wasn't a good thing, but a lot worse things could happen, too. It's all part of the code that all SEALs live by. But Horace couldn't shake the feeling that he hadn't been there for Mark, or that if he had been there, perhaps…just maybe…things might have gone differently. Eventually, he realized that was arrogant. Mark had been surrounded by other SEALs just as capable as Horace. But the hole in soul didn't go away. What the hell?

Eventually, he stopped by one of the forward combat psychological units down range for a chat with someone in the hopes that they could help him figure it out. He was assigned to an Army Major who was a woman on her first deployment to a combat theater who had a degree in social work. Somehow, Horace didn't think this was going to go so well. Just the same, he was getting pretty sick of that hole in the pit of his stomach and not being able to get Mark out of his mind. So what the heck did he have to lose?

The talk with the Major wasn't an instant cure. Horace continued to struggle with mourning and grief issues triggered by Mark's death for several more months, but a lot of what the Major pointed out to Horace – what she helped him discover about himself in the forty-five minutes or so they spent together – was that the hole in his soul was bigger than Mark Rizzolo. Rizz was just the "trigger." Rizz represented to Horace all of the friends, teammates, and loved ones he had lost over the years and suppressed the natural grief cycle and mourning process that regular humans go through when they lose someone they are close to, let alone someone they care about. His best friend Rizz had died when Horace wasn't there to say good-bye, and there had been no psychological closure. So Hall of the unfinished emotional business that warriors repress in their psyches in order to keep on keeping on was seeping through the open doorway named Mike Rizzolo. So Horace put in for a few days of leave the next time they rotated back to the states and went to visit Rizz's family and his grave, where he said his proper farewells. After that, the hole in his soul began to heal.

Now, since he had been forced to retire due to the severity of his injuries, a similar hole had opened up and was gnawing away at him. He missed the teams. He missed the missions. He missed the action, the knowledge, and the toys. When you're a SEAL in the Global War on Terror, you can't help but feel pretty significant in the world. You and your teammates are often caught in the crosshairs of history. You live on the tip of the spear of the most powerful nation in the history of the world. Then, one day, they hand you a piece of paper and flag and say, "Thanks, Chief, have a nice life," and it's all gone the next morning when you wake up. You're just a normal dude on the street with a modest pension, a DD214, and some cool T-shirts. You even have to get permission from some idiot with about one percent of your skills and qualifications and pay big fees if you still want to be able to carry a pistol for self-defense! It's easy to understand how it happened in retrospect, but Horace was still caught off guard when the sense of loss and grief returned.

# Chapter II:  Fish

*"If people concentrated on the really important things in life, there'd be a shortage of fishing poles."  ~ Doug Larson*

The motor slowed and the flats skiff gently came off of plane, nudging Horace out of his introspection.

"We're here.  Just sit tight and keep your eyes open, because we're going to have to look for them.  We might have to wait and we might have to hunt a bit, but they're here, Horace.  There have been over a thousand juvenile tarpon – mostly in the forty to eighty pound range in this area Hall week…and they're not going anywhere else for awhile," instructed Captain Hal with a smile on his face that told Horace he meant every word of it.  Horace's plan for today was still on track.

Horace had learned a lot about Tarpon and how to catch them in just a few trips with Captain Hal since he moved in to the quaint roadside pay-by-the-week motel with a few cottages and housekeeping apartments in Englewood, Florida.  The owners of the motel were really nice folks, a veteran of Korea and Vietnam and his German wife who had purchased the old fishermen's camp after retiring from the Army in the 1970s.  They had put a lot of tender loving care into the property over the years and it was a slice of Old Florida history and charm maintained with a mix of German pride and Army NCO efficiency.  It was modest, humble, comfortable, clean, and affordable.  Best of Hall, it was quiet and everyone respected one another's privacy.  They had recommended Captain Hal to Horace when he asked them about fishing guides.  They told Horace to drive down to the gas station early in the morning and look for the sea green Action Craft boat and gray GMC truck.  Then they gave Horace a good description of Captain Hal and told him that he would like him with a knowing smile.  Their advice was worth its weight in gold. You don't get that from a slick concierge desk brochure at the Hilton, and no tip was necessary.

Tarpon have a life cycle roughly the same as humans. A "juvenile" tarpon in the forty to eighty pound range is a teenager – likely between ten and fourteen years old. Like teenagers, they tend to be a bit more aggressive, less wary, and more athletic than older Tarpon. This combination makes for great sport for fly and light tackle anglers who enjoy sight-fishing for large, athletic fish. Similar to teenagers, they tend to run and feed in large groups rather than staking out solitary feeding or resting lies like some large ambush predators do. So when you find them, the action can get hot and heavy for awhile with several shots and a number of hook-ups on big, fast, high-jumping fish. Landing just one out of about seven you hook on a fly means you're a pretty good Tarpon angler. Most fly anglers consider "jumping" a Tarpon to be a success. "Jumping" a Tarpon means that the fish has taken your fly and you've gotten a hook set well enough in the beast that it runs for a bit and then makes its first aerial leap. That's how sporty fishing for Tarpon on a fly rod is. It isn't easy. They're not easy to cast to. They aren't easy to hook well, because they have exceptionally hard mouths. And they're extremely powerful, fast, and intelligent fish. So they're far more difficult to land than most fish. That is why they have earned their nickname among anglers: the Silver King! Among saltwater fly anglers, landing a one hundred pound class Tarpon is generally considered the apex of the sport.

Unlike so many other types of fishing, though, fly fishing isn't really just about the end goal of boating fish. Far more of the emphasis and enjoyment of fly fishing lies in the pursuit of the quarry, the thrill of the chase, the camaraderie amongst the anglers for whom it is their life's passion, and the arts and crafts that are such an integral part of the sport than is to be found in other methods of fishing. This fullness of the experience – the inter-connectedness of such a variety of things from crafts like fly tying to boats and a sort of kinship among the anglers that reminded him a bit of the brotherhood within the SEALs is what drew Horace to fly fishing like a moth to a flame. It was the only thing he had found since leaving the Navy that engaged so many aspects of his being for a single purpose. Maybe it was just fishing, and it certainly wasn't chasing dangerous terrorists around the world, but it engaged his mind, body, and soul in a multi-faceted way and plugged him in to nature and a community like nothing else he had found since he had been amputated from the SEALs he so dearly loved.

No Tarpon were going to have to die today, either. No Tarpon was in any way likely to kill Horace or the Captain out here on the calm waters of Charlotte Harbor. This game was just for kicks and nobody had to get hurt. For Horace, that was a huge bonus! After a lifetime of destruction and danger, the innocence of fishing was incredibly refreshing and uplifting – soothing and healing ointment to his wounded soul. The ability to hunt, capture, and then release his prey unharmed into the wild with a "thanks for playing" was almost magic to a guy like Horace. He was certain that most people could never appreciate just how special it was to him, and he never spoke a word about it to anyone. Some things, like the satisfaction a nation's top-tier warrior takes in the job well done when he kills his nation's enemy as ordered, are just better left unsaid. Unless you have been there and done that, it is impossible to comprehend the mixed emotions and their intensity – how simultaneously contradictory and clarifying that experience can be. Talking about it will only lead to misunderstandings. For all of the times Horace had felt the exhilarating satisfaction of success, snatching victory out of the jaws of defeat, triumphing over evil, and saving innocence from tyranny, he had never escaped the horrible responsibility and pangs of sadness that accompany having to take another person's life. In fact, the more formidable an adversary was, the greater the warrior's respect for them naturally became. When the end finally came for Horace's enemies, some sense of loss was inescapable. Nobody wants to hear about this stuff. This is why they pay other people to do it for them. That's why he grinned ear to ear and his soul sang a silent song of triumph that he couldn't explain to anyone each time he caught and released a quality fish after a great battle and watched as it swim away. He no longer had to kill his competition. There had been enough dying for one lifetime.

"There they are. I'm going to ease over there, Horace. Grab that sinking line rod with the big purple fly on it and get ready," Captain Hal said in a voice full of excitement and suddenly taught with an edge of seriousness. The captain now had his "game face" on, a combination of playful joy and hardcore seriousness that was rare outside the SpecOps community. The guide obviously loved his work and had a strong work ethic. He wanted to perform at his peak all the time – the hallmark of a real winner. The self-confident way Hal carried himself and communicated with others told an unmistakable tale of a life lived achieving the goals he set for himself. But when he got on fish, he took on a boyish enthusiasm that gave away his passion for fishing – especially Tarpon fishing.

Horace carefully removed the heavy, one-piece fly rod from the rack under the gunwale of the skiff. He moved to the bow of the boat. Standing in the forward end of the cockpit below the casting deck, he unhooked the fly and stripped out about sixty feet of fly line, letting it coil neatly beside his bare feet. As Captain Hal gently moved the boat into the spot where they would begin their wind-pushed drift into the rolling Tarpon, Horace double-checked his hat, sunglasses, shirt, and pants to ensure he was squared away. Murphy says that if something can snag a fly line it will snag a fly line, and a fly line wrapped around anything when a Tarpon takes off after being hooked is in serious trouble! These fish will pull grown men out of the boat and into the water. They will take off fingers caught in fishing line. Wrap a fly line around your ankle when a big Tarpon takes your fly and you may lose your foot. These fish are strong, ferocious, smart, and have amazing reserves of endurance. Being dragged by the ankle or wrist through shark-infested waters by a big Tarpon after whacking your head on the edge of the boat as the fish pulled you overboard is not a good career move!

Captain Hal had slowed the boat to a creep using the trolling motor. He was just about where he wanted to be, directly upwind of the pod of Tarpon. Horace watched the Silver Kings roll on the surface, one after another, as he and the captain made their final approach. Captain Hal was giggling now.

"This is gonna be great!" the captain said quietly as he shut off the trolling motor. "I don't want to push in too close, Horace, these guys don't like trolling motors. We'll let the wind push us down to the fish from here."

"Aye, aye, Skipper," Horace said with a grin tossed back over his shoulder to his guide.

"I know you can just jump in there, swim one of these fish down, and wrestle it into submission with your bare hands, but please try to stay in the boat this time. Okay?" Captain Hal was grinning. He had a very complimentary way of teasing people that Horace thought must pay off in better tips from his customers. The last time Horace had gone fishing with Captain Hal, he lost his balance while standing on the forward casting deck at the bow of the boat while it sat motionless on a shallow flat. They were fishing for Sea Trout and Redfish. Rather than risk injury by trying to catch himself and keep from going into the water, Horace just let himself fall – and pushed away a bit to clear the boat. He landed in the shallow water with a huge splash to avoid hitting the bottom with breakable body parts – hands, wrists, elbows, toes, ankles, and head. As soon as Horace had indicated he was alright, Hal began laughing hysterically and teasing him for diving in to such shallow water. Hall of the usual jibes about scaring off Hall the fish and scoring a 7.5 for the dive due to a sloppy water entry followed before Horace even got back on board and put himself back together. Horace was laughing too. Shit happens! The difference between a world-class athlete and a regular Joe isn't whether or not they fall now and then. The difference is seen by the fact that athletes rarely get hurt when they fall, and they collect themselves and recover quickly. Nobody ever got to be great at anything without screwing up. If you can't laugh at your own frailties and mistakes, you are taking things way too seriously.

"In the boat, Aye, Captain!" Horace said with a grin.

"If things get too sporty up there and you want me to come hold you by the belt to keep you in, just holler," Captain Hal continued to tease as they closed the last few yards to get in to casting distance of the edge of the pod of Tarpon.

"The first one you see roll within casting distance is yours, Horace," said the captain. That was his way of saying it was game on!

Horace slowed his breathing and relaxed his muscles by taking a few long, deep breaths and consciously relaxing each hand, arm, leg, and his back. Once an angler deploys his slack line at his feet, he must not move his feet. The best way to foul a fly line laying on the deck is to move a foot, either stepping on or through the coils of fly line. You can move anything else, but the rod and your feet need to remain as motionless as possible.

The wait was not long. The anticipation was always palpable. In these moments, a person becomes fully alive.

"There's your fish!" exclaimed the captain.

The unmistakable roll of the Tarpon appeared without a sound and vanished fifty feet in front of the boat. Horace had already dangled the fly in the water long enough to get it soaked. He quickly rolled the fly, leader, and first ten feet or so of line forward off the bow, picked it up off the water immediately, and took it into a back cast. One false cast forward, slipping line to add weight beyond the tip of the rod, and a second back cast to load the rod happened in three seconds. The presentation cast was smooth and relaxed, accelerating from slower to faster as the rod moved toward the target. Horace hauled on the sinking line in his left hand and stopped the rod at a point at a ten o' clock angle in front of himself, aiming just a couple of feet above where he wanted the fly to enter the water – a spot just beyond where the Tarpon had surfaced. As he released the line with his left hand just as the bent fly rod was stopping, the slack line at his feet quickly shot up through his open fingers and the rod guides. The fly landed within a foot of where Horace had aimed it.

"Let it sink," Captain Hal reminded him.

Horace counted to seven as he stood motionless in the boat, fly rod in hand.

"Now strip – slowly now, Horace," the guide coached from the stern of the boat.

Tucking the fly line under the first two fingers on his rod hand, Horace pulled straight back with his left hand on the line smooth and slow. He continued this pull as far as he could comfortably reach. Dropping the slack line, he reached forward to where the fly line came out from under the fingers of his right hand and began to repeat the retrieve.

After about six inches, the line went taught. The fly wouldn't budge. Fish!

"Strike! Strike! Strike!" exclaimed Captain Hal in his powerful baritone.

Horace bore down on the fly line in his left hand and released the line from under the fingers on his right hand as he yanked hard with his left, pointing the rod tip straight at the spot where the line disappeared in the water. The big fish took line, but Horace knew not to give it up without a fight. He held on to the fly line with a vice-like grip as the Silver King in front of the boat invisibly engaged in this tug-o-war. After a couple of seconds, the big fish won and the slack line shot through Horace's fingers until it was all gone. Now the fish was on the reel.

"Keep that rod tip down and hit him three times…hard!" coached the captain.

Horace had already started moving before Hal stopped giving instructions. With the rod tip angled toward the water, he re-captured the fly line against the fly rod's cork grip and yanked back hard against the fish. The rod bent sharply, but deep into the thick part of the rod above the grip. He repeated the move two more times. The third time, the line shot out from under his fingers in spite of his best grip and the Tarpon took off like a rocket away from the fishermen. The reel was spinning fast and singing that distinct song of fish tearing line off the spool at a high rate of speed.

"Keep that rod low and the fight in the butt, Horace!" shouted Captain Hal from the stern of the boat.

Horace did as he was told; keeping pressure on the fish, but with the rod low to the water and the bend as deep into the thickest part of the fly rod as possible.

The last of the one hundred ten feet of fly line disappeared and fluorescent orange Dacron backing shot off the reel and out through the guides of the fly rod. The Tarpon was still underwater and running hard, but the angle was changing as the fish put distance between itself and the boat. From Horace's perspective, he had a hard time discerning the depth of the fish.

"He's coming up!" shouted the guide.

The moment that every saltwater fly rodder lives for is the moment a nice Tarpon goes airborne with your fly lodged firmly in its mouth. This is called "jumping a Tarpon." When these massive fish leap into the air there is nothing between man and fish but a tiny piece of string. Such a large and beautiful fish jumping into the air is a spectacle, but watching and hearing it happen while you hold on to a fishing rod at the other end of the line is electric! The fish's incredible speed and power are telegraphed back via the line and the rod. The angler can feel it. It is awesome. No matter who you are, where you're from, or what you have done up until that very moment, you feel as if you've met your match.

Time began to move in slow-motion. For Horace, this was a familiar sensation. Decades of adrenaline-charged exposure to high risk situations had transformed Horace's mind in to an organ with two operating speeds: normal and what he called "Oh Shit!" mode. The warrior-turned-fisherman was quite comfortable in this high-speed mental state. New research by a neuroscientist named David Eagleman and University of Manchester professor Steve Taylor scientifically documented this phenomenon and put forth theories for how and why it happens. These experts believe that time is perceived by human beings in relation to the amount of activity in the brain. During times of extremely high synaptic exchange of neurons in the brain, what some may call "sensory overload," the human perception of time slows even though real time remains constant. Think of it like watching the world go by through the window of a train. If the train is moving slowly, the

24

world seems relaxed and normal. If the train is moving at high speed, the world rushes by outside in a blur. Within minutes, the passenger looking out the window will begin to notice more and more detail as the high-speed train rumbles through the world around it. But the objects being viewed by the passenger aren't behaving any differently than usual, and the train is moving at the same high rate of speed. The person's perception becomes better defined, but nothing else changes. Eagleman's research using free-fall experiments proved that the vast majority of participants significantly over-estimated the amount of time they were in the air after falling off of a high platform and landing in a safety net below.

The Tarpon leapt from the water at full speed, but to Horace it rose out of the sea and into the air in slow-motion. Rolling onto its left side, the great fish crashed back to the surface in a tremendous splash.

When a Tarpon jumps, the angler has to be careful not to raise the rod instinctively, but to dip the rod lower and forward in an attempt to create a bit of slack in the line between the fish and the fisherman. This slack absorbs the shock of this violent action, allowing for a better chance for the hook to remain embedded in the Tarpon's thick, cartilage-like plates inside its mouth. But many Tarpon throw the hook on the first leap, in spite of the best efforts of world-class anglers. Staying hooked up to a Tarpon after this jump is the critical difference between hooking one and landing one. Captain Hal said that if you could stay hooked up to a Tarpon for the first thirty seconds, you had a very good chance of landing it. That, Horace had learned, was a very big "if!"

"Rod tip down! Rod tip down!" barked Captain Hal as the fish crashed back into the water.

"Reel, reel, reel!" he coached from behind the center console of the flats skiff.

Now Horace had to quickly take up the slack created by the momentum of the boat sliding along the surface, dragged by this mammoth fish, and the fish's sudden loss of forward momentum when he jumped.

25

"She's a bigger fish than I expected, Horace. I'll bet she's pushing a hundred thirty," exclaimed the captain.

One hundred thirty pounds? That isn't a juvenile Tarpon. That's an adult! That would mean this was most likely a resident adult, the wiliest of all the Tarpon in the vicinity of Boca Grande. Horace was determined to stay with her as long as possible. If fortune played their way just enough, the captain and Horace would get some nice photos of a trophy class Tarpon alongside the boat. But he also knew all too well that landing a one hundred thirty pound adult Tarpon was a whole different ballgame than landing forty pound juveniles. Keeping a strong bend in the rod, Horace reeled against the monster every chance he got.

Captain Hal was now occupied with steering the boat and keeping a little more drag on the fish to help wear it out by using the weight and resistance of the boat against the fish's will. Keeping the boat at an angle behind the fish as she swam for open water required a lot of attention. Too much pressure and she would come unbuttoned. A broken leader, a bent hook, a failed knot in the line is all it would take. One wrong move or waiting too long to move would spell the end for Horace's fish. Hal was determined to do all he could to help Horace land his first big Tarpon on a fly rod. He kept one hand on the wheel and one on the throttle; both eyes on the fish he and Horace were chasing across Charlotte Harbor this glorious late Summer morning.

The two men really weren't gaining any line on this big Tarpon, and she didn't seem to be wearing down very quickly. Ten minutes and another jump had passed, and Horace was still hooked up to this glorious fish. They had definitely survived those first thirty seconds. According to Captain Hal, the possibility of landing this Tarpon were now pretty good. But one mistake that put too much slack in the line or applied too much pressure for the tackle to bear would bring the whole glorious struggle to a sudden end.

You have to stay alert and focused when battling big fish, especially on fly tackle from a small flats boat.

Horace had heard stories of epic battles with Tarpon just a bit larger than this one that had taken a couple of hours. In fact, Hal had told him the story of his biggest solo-caught Tarpon, the one that convinced the salty sea captain to never fish solo for trophy Tarpon again. Six hours later, the Captain said, he laid bloody and delirious, totally exhausted and dehydrated, on the bow of his skiff. He had no idea where he was and he had lost a $900 fly rod and $600 reel to the ocean. He landed and released a two hundred pound Tarpon, but he lost the rod and reel overboard sometime during the release. The sun was about to drop below the horizon, and Hal had to gather himself together enough to figure out where he was and take the boat in to the nearest marina. He needed medical attention.

The story had run in the region's newspapers, complete with photos that Horace had seen already. Captain Hal was off the water for weeks afterward as he recuperated, and his boat had required over a thousand dollars worth of repairs. He filed an insurance claim for the rod because that was accidental, but the boat repairs had to be paid for out of pocket. At any time, Captain Hal could have cut the line and disengaged from the giant Tarpon. But he had succumbed to "Tarpon Fever," and was compelled to fight this fish of a lifetime to the bitter end. So the damages weren't accidental. They were willful and the cost was "on him."

Hal said his medical expenses added another four hundred dollars to the bill for his "bucket list" achievement. Hall totaled, including lost charters during his recuperation, he figured that fish cost him almost eight thousand dollars – net…after Hall was said and done…real cash out of his bank account. Horace had asked Hal if it was worth it when Hal told him the story. The old captain grinned, stared Horace in the eyes, and said, "Yes. That and more, but I'll never try it again. I almost died a couple of times that day. I'm too old to tempt fate like that more than once."

Horace knew that a one hundred thirty pound Tarpon was not in the same league as a two hundred pound "senior citizen of The Pass," but he knew Hal would enjoy landing this fish Almost as much as he did, himself. He kept hearing Captain Hal's voice echoing in his mind: just stay connected. Just stay connected. Now it took careful persistence to wear a Tarpon down without allowing it to spit out the hook, break the line, or foul the line on something. It was all about keeping good tension on the fish within the tackle's tolerances, and trying to keep the fish in open water. Then, of course, you had to hope a shark didn't attack it.

Sharks love Tarpon. Experts say that if you fish for Tarpon much, it is just a matter of time until a big shark takes one away from you. As a general rule of thumb, the old salts say, "Where there are Tarpon, there are sharks."

"We've been on this fish for over thirty minutes, Horace," Captain Hal's voice ruptured the veil of determination and concentration that had enveloped him. "You're in good shape. She should start to wear down pretty soon."

The Tarpon was now swimming around below the surface without jumping at a range of about sixty or seventy feet from the boat. It would occasionally take an additional fifty feet or so of line, but then Horace would reel that back in as soon as the surge in energy from the fish subsided. His arms and stomach were beginning to feel the strain. He could tell he would end up with a tender spot on his shins just below the knees where he kept bouncing them off of the back edge of the casting deck or the gunwale of the boat. He could feel the sun on his nose and neck, the early symptom of impending sunburn. He had forgotten to put on any sunscreen. He was already sweating freely, and rivulets of sweat were pooled in the bottom rims of his sunglasses. The small flats skiff was almost a half mile closer to the center of the bay than where Horace had hooked this fish.

"This is amazing, Hal," Horace called back over his shoulder to his guide.

"This is what we live for, Horace," chuckled the charter captain from behind the console of his boat. "Just keep the slack out and don't forget to bow to her if she jumps. Keep that rod tip down. You're doing great."

Captain Hal had literally taken at least a thousand different people Tarpon fishing on these waters. His love affair with sport-fishing began when he was a teenager, when he spent the summer after his sixteenth birthday crewing aboard a sport-fishing charter boat out of San Diego. Nearly fifty years later, the Captain had just about seen every kind of fisherman and every sort of human behavior one might imagine on the water. He and his clients had boated nearly every species of sport and game fish from the Pacific Coast to the Atlantic Coast, Alaska to Florida, Mexico to Bermuda and the Cayman Islands. In all of years of fishing, he had never met an angler quite like Horace. Standing more than six feet tall, lean, and hard as nails, Horace MacDonald was a perfect example of vitality and athleticism. Nonetheless, two decades of very hard wear and tear had taken a toll on Horace's incredible athleticism. Hal had gotten a couple of glimpses into the chinks in Horace's formidable armor. Once, when Horace lost his balance and fell off the bow of the boat while they were sitting in calm water, and another time when he saw him stiffen and take in a sharp breath in reaction to pain while he was simply climbing into the driver's seat of his Scout. His injured leg had given out unexpectedly and Horace grabbed hard to the steering wheel with his right hand while steadying himself against the edge of the seat with his left hand pressed firmly on the arm rest of the driver's side door. Captain Hal started to move to grab his younger fishing buddy, but pulled up short when it dawned on him that Horace seemed to have gotten it under control and rushing to his aid to prop him up would likely embarrass him. Hal knew it would embarrass him if the roles were reversed. He could imagine how much more awkward it would be for a former Navy SEAL more than twenty years his junior to be steadied and helped into his truck by a much older man. Instead, he asked, "You got it, Horace?"

"Yeah," grimaced the young veteran, "Damned leg gave out – but I'm fine. Thanks."

And with that Horace slid behind the wheel of his old Scout II. The two men said their farewells as Horace started the engine, and he drove off back toward the roadside motel up Placida Road.

Horace still had very quick reactions and remained physically formidable in spite of his life-threatening injuries. Hal had noticed that the younger man was extremely aware of his surroundings and possessed an uncanny sense of direction and location. The Captain had never had to show his newest "regular customer" a map, not even using the GPS unit on his boat. Horace always seemed to know exactly where he was and had accurate and detailed maps of the area stored in his head. Captain Hal had been impressed with Horace's detailed knowledge of local geography and history from the first time they met, which was within two weeks of the younger man's arrival in the area.

Horace wasn't from here. Heck, he wasn't even from Florida. Hal had learned that Horace grew up in a small town in Texas. But he knew the topography, history, and most important businesses and property owners as if he had been born and raised here. When Captain Hal had pointed out the DuPont family estate on Gasparilla Island, Horace looked and then said, "So the Russell's home must be about a mile south of here," as if it were half question and half statement of fact. Of course, he was right. The Russell family, with two governors and two Presidents among a father and his sons, had a large family estate in the heart of Boca Grande. They were an avid fishing, sailing, and golfing family with estates on the coast of Maine, here in Boca Grande, and in Texas and Colorado. The family money came from the oil and gas industry prior to the elder Russell's foray into politics that landed him in the White House. Hal was surprised than a newcomer would know such a detail of local geography, because Boca homeowners tend to keep a fairly low profile. Apparently, Horace had done his homework before deciding to come here.

Hal rarely had to tell Horace anything twice. In his role as a fishing guide, Captain Hal had long ago developed quite the habit of repeating the fundamentals over and over again to his customers. On about their third fishing outing, Hal noticed that Horace always seemed to be doing what he was about to remind him to do. Sometimes, he would say it anyway. Other times, he would bite his tongue and replace instruction with encouragement or a compliment. This guy was a very quick learner who could translate new knowledge into physical skills faster than anyone Hal had ever met. It impressed him. In fact, he was a bit jealous…in a good way. Captain Hal counted it as good fortune when he got a client half as capable as Horace MacDonald. Yet, he knew Horace needed some help now and then due to his injuries. And he always kept a close eye on Horace when they were together, ready to lend a strong hand in any moment of need. He like Horace right away, and he took a strong personal interest in helping Horace to succeed – whatever that word meant to new friend. The Captain wasn't quite sure what Horace was really doing here. Was he merely here to fish? Was he fishing to pass the time while he waited for something – or someone? Captain Hal read something that the famous American naturalist author, Henry David Thoreau, had written that always echoed in his mind when he thought of Horace.

*"Some men fish all their lives without knowing it is not the fish they are after."*

Captain Hal was pretty sure that Horace knew, but he had no idea what that might be. He wasn't going to ask him, either.

"She's gonna jump!" shouted the Captain.

And with that the Tarpon broke the surface, ripping the fly line clear of the water just as Horace leaned forward and dipped the rod tip, poking it straight toward the fish.

"That's it, Horace! Way to go! Just stay connected, buddy. You've got this fish if we can stay with her," exhorted Captain Hal.

"Beautiful! Just fuckin' beautiful!" shouted Horace into the sea breeze.

"She's got to start wearing out soon. We can't let up on her or she'll get a second wind," the Captain explained to his star pupil above the sound of idling engine and the sounds of the bay.

"I don't know who is wearing out faster, Hal. Her or me?" shouted back the Navy veteran.

The Captain just laughed. He was pretty sure that there was no quitting in this man. He knew Horace was used to winning and didn't have a word for surrender in his mental vocabulary. But he understood the

31

sentiment Horace had expressed, and the things that go through a man's mind when he's hooked up to a Silver King this size.

The visceral sense of the power and athleticism of a Tarpon gets transmitted very efficiently from leader to fly line to the tip of the rod an angler is holding on to, and it is an awe-inspiring sensation. Tarpon can reach speeds approaching thirty-five miles per hour during a run, and they accelerate from zero to thirty in the time it takes to draw a full breath. They can swim for days without ceasing at five miles per hour. These characteristics, combined with their beauty, strong schooling tendencies, acrobatic nature when hooked, abundance in shallow water, and willingness to take an artificial lure, put the Tarpon on top of the list of most sought-after species of fish by in-shore saltwater fishermen in the world's warm climates from the West coast of Africa to Central and North America. Tarpon are splendid creatures that trigger both adrenaline rushes and endorphin releases from the most seasoned anglers. Thousands of these sportsmen and women travel to Boca Grande annually for a chance to dance with a Silver King.

# Chapter III:  Shockwaves

*"All that is necessary for evil to flourish is for good men to do nothing." ~ Edmund Burke*

Horace was aware of a few other boats in the vicinity, but he was relying upon his teammate – his guide – to pilot the boat.  That meant that Captain Hal was primarily responsible for safe navigation, allowing Horace to focus on fighting the big fish on the rod and reel.  But years of situational awareness training and the life-or-death games of Horace's former occupation had honed his peripheral vision, hearing, and attention to detail to a razor's edge that would not quickly grow dull.  He had caught a glimpse of the big cabin cruiser and sub-consciously estimated its range and bearing to be seven hundred meters or so to their right-front.  His focus never left the massive silver fish at the end of his line.  Old habits die hard.  He noticed two people on the deck:  an adult male and probably a younger male or female, but he paid them no attention.

Horace felt the shockwave before he saw or heard the explosion.  His ears detected the sudden change in pressure and the boat's fiberglass hull trembled under his bare feet for a split-second before the sound wave reached him just as he became conscious of the flash in his peripheral vision.  Battlefield instincts kicked in automatically and Horace dropped to his knees and ducked his head, all the while keeping tension on the rod in his hands.  Stealing a quick glance toward the blast, he saw that the large cabin cruiser was gone – replaced by a large, burning slick, a cloud of smoke and flame roiling in the air above it, and a debris field fluttering high into the air and landing on the water at least one hundred yards closer to his position than the boat had been a second before.  Glancing quickly aft, he saw that Captain Hal was dialing his cell phone and noticed the look of shock and concern on his face.

"Use the radio!" shouted Horace over his shoulder.  Cellular phone connections were very good on Charlotte Harbor, but a lot of first responders would be monitoring the primary ship-to-shore emergency VHF radio frequency directly.  Horace knew that the few minutes difference it would take to engage a 9-1-1 operator and dispatchers for the various agencies with jurisdiction could  mean life or death to whomever was on board that boat.  Without even thinking about it, Captain Hal set his phone down and picked up the microphone for his on board VHF marine radio.  His other hand turned the radio on and switched the frequency quickly to the local emergency frequency.  Horace heard the radio crackle, but no one was talking yet.

"U.S. Coast Guard…U.S. Coast Guard…or any station, this is Captain Hal White.  Do you copy?"

Letting his thumb off the microphone's push-to-talk key, Hal paused only for a second of white noise before a clear, powerful female voice replied, "Captain, this is the U.S. Coast Guard helicopter out of Fort Myers, Florida.  We read you loud and clear, Captain.  What is your emergency, over?"

"U.S. Coast Guard, we just observed an explosion on board a boat near our location.  We are requesting immediate assistance.  The boat is gone…," the Captain trailed off and let his thumb off of the key on the mic.

"Captain, what is your name and current location, over?" asked the Coast Guard chopper.

Captain Hal looked around quickly to get his bearings, then remembered to check the GPS-enabled sonar plotter on his dash board.

"U.S. Coast Guard, my current position is latitude north twenty-six degrees fifty-one point eight seven minutes by longitude west eighty-two degrees four point one five minutes, over. Oh yeah, my name is Captain Hal White."

There was several seconds of dead air before the Coast Guard helicopter responded, "Captain, how many persons do you have on board, over?"

Hal quickly responded, "Two...two adult males."

"Are you wearing life jackets, captain, over?" asked the female on board the Coast Guard helicopter.

"No...uh, negative, over."

"Captain, do you have two life jackets on board, over?" asked the female voice over the radio.

"Affirmative. Yet we do," replied the Captain. "Horace, the life jackets are in the bow hatch below your feet. You're going to have to break that fish off somehow and get them for us. We're going in."

"The Tarpon is already gone, Captain. Life jackets, aye!" replied Horace. As soon as he had told Captain Hal to use the radio instead of the phone, Horace had locked down the drag on the fly reel and grabbed the line with the hand he was using to hold the rod. Bracing the reel hard against his stomach so that it would not turn, he pulled hard against the fish of his dreams. The fish came up after about three seconds, leapt into the air, and shaking its head violently it had thrown the hook as Horace raised the rod tip to maintain full tension. Horace had already reeled in the fifty or so feet of line, and was just moving to stow the rod when Captain Hal spoke to him about the life jackets.

"To Hell with the rod, Horace. Just drop it in the deck," barked Captain Hal.

Horace dropped the rod into the main cockpit of the boat with a thud and turned to the bow hatch to retrieve two life jackets. Opening the hatch, he also found a bow line, a throw buoy, and a first aid kit that he pulled out with the life jackets. Then he stepped back into the cockpit

35

to the center console and handed a life jacket to Captain Hal. He put one of them on and tightened it down.

"I haven't worn one of these in years," Horace said with a quick smile to his friend and guide. "I got the throw buoy, some extra line, and the first aid kit out of the hatch, too."

"Good," said the Captain.

"Captain Hal, Captain Hal, this is the U.S. Coast Guard helicopter out of the Punta Gorda station. Do you read me, over?"

"Yes, I read you, Coast Guard," replied the fishing guide.

"Captain, I want you and your passenger to put on those life jackets, over," instructed the woman in the helicopter.

"Affirmative, Coast Guard. My passenger and I both have on life jackets now, over," replied Captain Hal.

"Captain Hal, this is US Coast Guard, do you have emergency equipment on board your vessel, over?" asked the now-familiar voice of the female Coast Guardsman.

"Affirmative, Coast Guard. We have throw buoys, lines, fire extinguishers, and first aid supplies on board, over," responded the Captain.

"Good, Captain. I'm glad to hear it. We are en route to your location, but we are approximately seven minutes away. Under maritime law I am instructing you to attempt to render immediate aid to any souls you find alive from the distressed vessel. Do you understand, Captain?"

"Affirmative, Coast Guard, I understand and will comply, over."

"Captain, before you head in there I need to make sure you understand a few things, over."

"Go ahead, Coast Guard," replied the former Marine NCO who suddenly felt like he was back in the rice paddies of South Vietnam talking to his platoon leader on the radio. Back in those days, he was

36

taking orders from kids his own age. This woman sounded pretty young compared to Captain Hal. The irony wasn't entirely lost to the gravity of the situation.

"Captain, I am instructing you not to endanger yourself, your passenger, or your vessel to render assistance. You are to only render whatever aid you feel that you can safely execute. Do you understand, over?" instructed the Coast Guard lady.

"Affirmative, Coast Guard. Safety first! I understand. But I should probably tell you that my passenger is retired Navy SEAL Chief Petty Officer Horace MacDonald, and I have been trained in advanced rescue, first aid, and CPR. I'm also an old Marine, young lady. We'll do what we can, over," explained Captain Hal with a wink and nod to Horace.

"That's good, Captain. Glad to know who we're working with. Stay safe and keep this radio channel open. Report what you find upon close inspection when you get a chance. This is US Coast Guard helicopter en route to your location, standing by. Go get 'em, gentlemen."

"Roger that, Coast Guard. We'll do what we can. See you soon. This is Captain Hal White standing by, over."

With that, Captain Hal set down the microphone and reached for the boat's wheel. He looked up at Horace and caught his gaze for a brief moment, man to man, before he said, "Horace, no hero stuff. Okay? We play this safe."

"Safety first, Captain, just like you told the Mud Ducks," Horace said without breaking eye contact.

"Then let's go see if there's anyone in that water. Have a seat," said Captain Hal as he reached for the throttle of his Action Craft Flyfisher.

Fishing was over for today. Men of the sea never refuse to stop and render aid to another vessel in trouble. That was the maritime law that the lady from the Coast Guard had mentioned. In an emergency, the U.S. Coast Guard can press into service any U.S. flagged vessel or foreign vessel in U.S. water. As a licensed charter boat captain, Hal had no legal choice but to assist in the rescue response. But he would have done it anyway.

With Horace seated in front of the console, the old charter guide eased into the throttle and pointed the bow of the seventeen foot flats skiff toward the burning debris field on the water some five hundred or so meters to his two o'clock. Silently, Hal hoped they would find someone to rescue, but he sort of doubted it. It had been a huge explosion.

"Hal, I smell Semtex!" shouted Horace over the engine noise when they were about one hundred meters from the debris field in the sea. Hal had already begun to slow the boat back down and come off plane when Horace spoke.

"What?" Hal shouted over the noise.

"Semtex. Plastic explosives, Captain. It has a very distinct smell," Horace explained loud and clear enough to be heard over the noise of the motor and the wind.

"Are you sure, Horace?" asked the Captain with an incredulous look on his face.

Hal's mind was buzzing now. He had seen a few ship-board fires and he knew people who had been killed in gas tank explosions aboard boats. Carelessness and sloppy repair habits were dangerous on the sea. Horace, being a Navy SEAL, was highly trained in demolitions and explosive materials. These guys were the best of the best, but plastic explosives? That would mean...

"Roger. I'm sure, Hal! SEALs and Tangos use that shit, and I've smelled more than my fair share. This was a bomb!" explained Horace, who was now scanning the debris field for signs of survivors or bodies floating in the water. He had tied a line to the pop-up cleat in the bow of the small boat and was standing in the cockpit on the main deck just behind the casting deck, holding the line in one hand to steady himself with a third point of contact with the boat. Hal hadn't even noticed when he did that.  In his other hand he held the throw bouy.  The fifty feet of line from the buoy coiled next to his bare feet.

What the Hell was he supposed to now, Hal wondered?  Should he report this to the Coast Guard?  Probably better to search for survivors now and report this to the investigators later, but were they in danger?  Hal wasn't sure.

"Horace, this is your domain now, buddy!  What should we do?" asked Captain Hal as the boat settled into a slow search pattern at the edge of the debris field.

"Search, Captain.  Search for survivors.  Take us in.  Stay away from the fire!"

With that, Captain Hal eased the boat into the edge of the debris field, heading straight to the place in the water where the boat had been not two minutes ago.  Any survivors would most likely be located near the middle.  If they didn't find anyone there, they would begin circling their way outward from the center.  But there was too much burning oil slick on the water at the center of the debris.  No one could survive in there anyway.  Slowly and carefully, scanning the water ahead and to each side of the light blue boat, Captain Hal headed into the heat and stench of the wreckage.

The first piece of debris that bounced off the hull of Hal's Action Craft boat gave him a shudder that ran up from the base of his spine to his neck.  The smell of burning diesel, saltwater, and something acrid in the mix that he couldn't identify assaulted his sense of smell.  He could taste it when he breathed.  He expected to find dead bodies, but no survivors.  This was a lot more than he expected when he left his home in Rotunda before dawn and headed for the gas station to go fishing.

"Body in the water!  Bearing: eleven o'clock.  Range: fifty meters," shouted Horace from the bow.

Instinctively, Hal turned the wheel and came onto the heading Horace had indicated.

"Alive or dead, Horace?" shouted Captain Hal.

"I don't know yet, Hal. No movement. Get me over there," shouted Horace.

The distinct thumping sound of the rotors of a U.S. Coast Guard Jayhawk helicopter approaching from the South suddenly pierced the edge of Horace's consciousness. "Good," he thought. "The Coasties will be here in about a minute."

Upon arrival, the Coast Guard chopper would first survey the wreckage. They'd pick out Hal's boat and make radio contact again. If there were bodies in the water, they'd deploy a rescue diver. Simultaneously, they would be coordinating with headquarters and first responders from the various law enforcement agencies that shared jurisdiction along the southern shoreline of Charlotte Harbor. Horace knew that was Lee County, and the nearest town was Punta Gorda. Florida Wildlife Commission might have a boat in the area, and local and county law enforcement and fire and rescue teams would be racing to the scene.

The body ahead of Horace and Hal was floating face down in the water and wasn't moving. Not a good sign that this person was still alive. But an unconscious person floats the same way. Horace noticed something about the body. Just under the surface, he could make out a shiny divers watch on the left wrist of the victim. The tattered remains of the person's shirt struck a familiar chord somewhere deep in Horace's memory banks, but he couldn't place it just yet. It was navy blue...a Polo or Nautica style windbreaker, popular among well-to-do sailors. It bore a logo Horace couldn't make out, but seemed familiar. He was scanning details in the immediate vicinity of the body for information that might be useful...clues to the crime that had obviously just been committed.

Hal maneuvered the boat slowly into position, bringing the body alongside the bow of his boat to where Horace could better figure out what they should do. As the body floated to within feet of the boat, Horace noticed that a large chunk of the back of the skull of what was obviously a middle-aged man was missing and blood flowed out into the sea water, staining a couple of feet of water around the man's head dark crimson. Then he recognized what was left of the jacket. The logo across the back was the Presidential Seal. Horace almost wretched. Releasing the line and the throw buoy, he leapt into the water instinctively. The life jacket popped him to the surface like a cork popping out of a champagne bottle. He turned around by scissor-kicking and twisting his torso in one forceful stroke, not even noticing the twinge of pain in his knee. And he was face-to-face with the mangled corpse of the former President of the United States, Greg R. Russell! Horace reached out one hand and lifted the President's head by the hair on top of his scalp. He saw something unexpected. A perfectly round entry wound in the President's forehead with burn stippling of the flesh on the President's face. He had been shot with a high caliber firearm at very close range…probably a pistol.

"Hal, help me get him out of the water! Move, dammit, move!" Horace hollered up at his friend in the boat.

Hals' voice shouted back down at him, "What the Hell do you think you're doing jumping in the water…" and then abruptly stopped as Hal's head and shoulders appeared above the gunwale of the boat.

"Is that…," Hal asked with a look of utter shock on his face.

"Yes, Hal, it's President Russell," shouted Horace. "Grab that line and help me get him aboard."

"Holy shit, Horace! What the fuck is happening?" exclaimed Captain Hal as he grabbed the bow line, released it from the cleat, and made ready with a bowline knot so Horace could slip a large loop of rope over the dead President's head and shoulders, secure it under his arms, and hoist him into the boat as Horace pushed from below.

"I don't know right now, Captain. I don't know. But you can bet your ass we're deep in the shit now, amigo!" Horace replied as he tread water and positioned the President's corpse to accept the rope Hal was fashioning.

Hal tossed the loop end of the rope to Horace. The former SEAL quickly slid the loop through the water and around the President's torso. He then tied the former politician's hands together in front of him at his waist by tucking them through his belt close together to hold his arms down as upward pressure was exerted on the rope.

"Ready, Hal!" shouted Horace.

Captain Hal strained against the rope as Horace kicked hard while holding the President's legs. He was able to raise the President's center of gravity to water level, and Hal hoisted the body aboard with a sickening thud.

"God dammit!" exclaimed the Captain.

"Shut that motor down so I can climb over the stern, Hal," shouted Horace from the bloody, debris-filled water.

"You got it, buddy," said the Captain as he moved to the console and hit the kill switch.

In seconds, Horace was back in the boat, soaking wet and breathing hard. His face, hands, and clothes were coated in a mix of diesel, sea water, and blood.

"What the Hell do we do now, Horace? He's dead as Hell!" asked Captain Hal.

"We keep searching, Captain. We keep searching."

"Captain Hal White, Captain Hal White, this is U.S. Coast Guard helicopter Fort Myers. Come in, over." The radio squalked loudly for the first time in several minutes, and Hal shifted behind the console and grabbed the microphone.

Looking at Horace he asked, "Do we tell them?"

"Hell yes, we tell them! This is no longer a typical Coast Guard rescue operation, Hal. This is a major national security incident! Welcome to the big show, my friend," responded Horace, who had already gotten his breathing under control and was busy reorganizing the lines and rescue gear.

Horace's mind was racing into high gear and the world around him was moving in slow motion. He was in the familiar "zone" of "Oh shit!" mode. With the rescue and safety gear squared away, he visually confirmed that his tackle bag was safely tucked away where he had stowed it, on the seat in front of the console. Who, why, and how questions were running through his mind and lists of likely answers were compiled and filed away for later reference in the blink of an eye. As he began to scan the water around the boat for anyone else, including the smaller person he had seen on board the President's boat, he began to assess the risk situation. Horace wasn't all that worried about the debris, flames, or smoke. He was pretty sure that Hal and he had that under control. They had fire extinguishers. The Coast Guard was on location. And Captain Hal was an able and safety conscious skipper with the judgment of a battle-hardened Marine who had spent his life at sea. What Horace was concerned about now was far more sinister and quite human in nature.

"U.S. Coast Guard this is Captain Hal White, over."

"Captain Hal, good to hear your voice again. This is U.S. Coast Guard. We are on scene and have visual contact with a light blue small craft in the debris field. Can you confirm that this is your vessel, over?"

"Roger, Coast Guard. That's us. This crazy SEAL jumped in the water to recover a body, Coast Guard, but we're fine. The body we recovered is not...I repeat...not fine, Coast Guard. He's dead. And you need to know who he is, Coast Guard," explained Captain Hal.

"Captain Hal, this is Coast Guard. Are you saying you have recovered a dead body from the wreckage, over?"

"Affirmative, Coast Guard. We have recovered one dead body, over," replied the old Vietnam veteran.

"Captain, this is Coast Guard. Did I understand that you have identified the body, over?" asked the female Coast Guardsman on board the helicopter.

"Affirmative, Coast Guard. We have positively identified the body of the person we have on board, over."

"Captain, do not…I repeat…do not identify this person via the radio. Do you understand, over?" ordered the lady in the Coast Guard chopper, with an edge of urgency discernible even via the radio.

"What do I do, Horace?" the Captain asked his fisherman-turned-recovery diver.

Horace turned where he stood on the bow casting deck, faced off toward Captain Hal who stood behind the center console, took a breath as he stared into Captain Hal's eyes directly, and said, "You tell them…and you repeat it three times very clearly: Phoenix One Down. Do you understand?"

"What the Hell? Is that some sort of code?" asked Captain Hal incredulously.

"Yes, Hal. That's exactly what it is. And they will know what it means," Horace explained. Then he barked, "Do it!"

Captain Hal only paused long enough to process how serious Horace had become. The initial insult of having orders barked to him by a client on his own boat faded in less than a heartbeat, and was replaced with the realization that this fisherman was a seasoned and senior Tier One special operator for the U.S. military. In less than a second, Hal realized what Horace had been talking about. He keyed the radio.

"Coast Guard this is Captain Hal White. I cannot comply. Phoenix One Down. I repeat, Phoenix One Down. Phoenix One Down. Do you copy?" the old Marine spoke slowly, clearly, and deliberately. Then he removed his thumb from the microphone and waited.

It seemed like several seconds passed with no reply from the Coast Guard chopper, which was now visible approaching at several hundred feet from the South…a bright orange and white whirlybird with a loud rotor wash underscored by the sound of turbine engines.

"Captain Hal, this is Coast Guard helicopter Fort Myers. Repeat your last, over."

"Coast Guard, this is Captain Hal White. We have both visually confirmed. Phoenix One Down, dammit!" a tear appeared in the corner of the big man's eye, and he quickly brushed it away.

"Captain Hal, can you please put Chief MacDonald on the radio, over?" the female voice of the Coast Guard pilot had softened noticeably, and it startled the old salty sea captain. Horace was moving toward the console immediately, and Hal handed him the mic. Then he swallowed the lump in his throat and stared at the dead former President bleeding all over the white deck of his boat. "How in the Hell did I get here?," he thought to himself.

"Coast Guard, this is Chief MacDonald. Go." Horace spoke into the radio. His voice was different; flat and emotionless. Hal noticed immediately.

"Chief, I need absolute confirmation and assurance on this. Do you copy?" came the reply from the Coast Guard chopper.

"Coast Guard helicopter Fort Myers, my call sign is…was…Reaper Six. I repeat: my call sign…Reaper Six. I confirm. Phoenix One Down, over. Now get it together, Ma'am, and let's do this," said Horace into the microphone. He glanced up toward the orange and white helicopter. Almost as an after-though, he keyed the mic again and said, "Coast Guard, he personally awarded me my Silver Star while I was in the hospital at Bethesda. I just went in the water and pulled his body on board this boat. It's him, dammit. And I smell Semtex all over this area. Do you read me, Coast Guard?"

There was a brief space of dead air on the radio. Then, "Chief, I copy ten by ten. Callsign Reaper Six acknowledged. Phoenix One Down. Phoenix One is down. Roger. Hang in there, Chief. You know all Hell is about to break loose, right?" the Coast Guard pilot's voice was now even softer than before…a clear note of concern in her voice.

"Roger that, Coast Guard. We're continuing to search for survivors until we receive further instructions. I counted two…I say again, two…souls on board the boat before the explosion, over," Horace explained into the mic.

"Copy that, Chief. Two souls observed on board. One recovered DOA. Recommence SAR, Chief. We'll support from the air and deploy my diver if needed, over."

"Roger, Coast Guard. This is Reaper Six, out."

"Chief, I mean Reaper Six! This is Coast Guard helicopter Fort Myers. I just need to say it. You served with my brother, Sammy. Copy?" said the voice from the sky.

Horace picked the mic back up, took a deep breath, and keyed the mic. "Roger that, Coast Guard. That would make you Lieutenant Sherrie Biggers. I wish we'd met under better circumstances, Lieutenant. But I'm glad to have a friendly on board right now. Reaper Six standing by."

Captain Hal had no idea what to think. There was a dead President in his boat with some kind of goddamned war hero frogman who was apparently in charge…or something like it. He calls himself "Reaper Six" and the whole damned Coast Guard knows who he is. "What the fuck is happening here? Is this some sort of dream…a bad flashback associated with a raging case of PTSD I didn't even know I had?" thought the old Marine turned fishing guide by way of a career in RV sales. "This is fucking crazy…like a Hollywood movie or something," Hal thought to himself as he listened to the conversation between the Coast Guard helicopter pilot and Horace unfold.

"Jeezus H. Christ, Horace. What the hell, man?" asked Captain Hal.

Putting his hand on his friend's shoulder, Horace looked him in the eye for the third time and said, "Captain, you're good to go. Don't sweat it, and follow my lead. We're a tight family nowadays and we just got a lucky draw of the cards. That Mud Duck pilot is the kid sister of one of the boys from my old Team. What's more, she flew twenty nine combat sorties as a Medevac pilot for the Army Reserve in Afghanistan a few years back. So she's good to go, too. Now, let's see if we can find any survivors. Okay?" and he smiled at the Captain and waited for his reply.

"It's been decades, Horace," Captain Hal said.

"Roger that, Captain. I thought I was done with this shit, too, my friend. Now let's saddle up and get the job done!"

"Okay. Get up there on the bow, Chief. Hang on. I'll try to steer clear of the fire, but take that extinguisher forward with you just in case. We're going home this afternoon. I'll be damned if I spend the night in the ER!" said Captain Hal as he put one hand on the wheel and one on the starter.

"Aye, aye, Captain! Let's find that kid or lady who I saw on the deck," Horace said as he grabbed the smaller fire extinguisher and headed for bow of the skiff. Now they were shouting over the noise of the Coast Guard helicopter, which was circling the debris field at a couple of hundred feet. No doubt, Lieutenant Sherrie Biggers had her hands full right about now on another frequency talking to her Air Traffic Control back in Fort Myers! They had probably heard everything, and the entire emergency management community would be kicking in to high gear. Homeland Security plans would be activated within minutes, and the airwaves, airspace, and water around here was about to get extremely crowded!

You just don't go around blowing up former Presidents of the United States of America while they're fishing in Boca Grande, Florida, for Pete's sake! Hal was still having a difficult time processing the mess he was unexpectedly in the middle of today. This stuff just doesn't happen in real life! Well, obviously, things had changed. This whole situation was extremely real and very much happening. Shit.

Hal and Horace combed the wreckage, smoke, and burning debris floating on the slick surface of Charlotte Harbor for several minutes, but found nothing.

Hal's cell phone rang. He answered the same way he always did.

"This is Captain Hal," he said as he held the phone to his ear. More bits of debris from the former President's fishing boat slid down the fiberglass side of Hal's skiff. He throttled down the engine to idle to hear whomever had called him.

"Captain, this is Special Agent in Charge Steve Purcell with the United States Department of the Treasury, Secret Service. Can you please confirm for me your full name, date of birth, and the city where you were born?" Alright. This was just too fucking crazy!

"You're who? How did you get my phone number?" asked the fishing guide.

"I said this is Special Agent in Charge Steve Purcell with the U.S. Secret Service. Please calm down and I'd like for you to positively ID yourself by telling me your full name, date of birth, and the city where you were born…please, Captain," the voice on the phone responded slowly, clearly, and very matter-of-factly.

"Horace, there's some guy on the phone who says he's with the Secret Service, and he wants my name, birthdate, and the city where I was born," Hal explained to Horace, who was standing with his back to Hal on the bow casting deck, scanning the water.

Without looking back, Horace hollered over his shoulder, "Tell him who you are and ask him what he wants."

Hal took the phone from his ear, shook his head, sighed deeply, and then replied, "This is Hal White. I run Boca Fly Fishing Charter Service out of Engleside, Florida. My date of birth is July nineteenth, nineteen fifty-eight. I was born in San Diego, California. What do you want from me…and how did you get my cell phone number?"

"Thanks Captain. I appreciate your cooperation. I don't know how I got your phone number, honestly, but I'm going to have to ask you to please hand the phone to Chief MacDonald," explained the voice on the other end of the line.

"Well I'll be goddamned! You listen to me, Special Agent in Charge whoever-the-hell you said you were. They call me Captain Hal because this is my boat. Capiche? I'm in charge on this boat no matter who my client is or whomever's dead body may be lying on my deck. You got that? We're sort of busy out here trying to find survivors and keep from dying ourselves. And I don't take orders from anybody when I'm standing on my own damned boat! So if you want something from me or Hor...I mean Chief MacDonald...you're gonna have to deal with me. Understand?" Captain Hal fumed into the phone.

"Okay, Captain. Okay. I hear you loud and clear and I'm not trying to run rough-shod over anyone. We need your help. I need your help. But right now...right this minute...I need a situation assessment that I can have a lot more confidence in if it comes from the Chief. That may not make sense to you, but that's reality, Captain. And I am depending on you to help me get the information I need so that I can help you, too. Please, Captain – please hand the phone to Chief MacDonald," the Secret Service agent explained into the phone.

"Horace, it's the Secret Service. They want to talk to you," shouted Captain Hal over the thump-thump-thump of the Coast Guard helicopter as it passed close enough by to stir the air, forcing Hal to grab the brim of his hat to keep it from flying off into the water.

"No dice, Captain! This is your boat and I'm just along for the ride. But you tell that suit on the phone to get his ass out here ASAP, and to bring everything he's got with him. Roger?" Horace shouted back over his shoulder again.

Overhead, Lieutenant Sherrie Biggers circled the HH-60 Jayhawk helicopter around the perimeter of the debris field at two hundred and sixty feet. From that vantage point, she could see the former Navy SEAL and the charter captain on board the small, light blue skiff with a white deck picking their way through the middle of the debris field from the explosion. She could see that the force of the explosion had distributed a debris field approximately one hundred meters in all directions from a burning oil slick in the center that must have been the approximate location of the boat when it exploded. Fuel explosions on board typical fishing vessels in these waters didn't throw debris more than a few yards from the boat. She had seen a couple of debris fields and wrecks from shipboard fires that had caused the fuel tanks to explode. They looked nothing like this. The ones she had seen before left a burning hull floating on the surface…in the process of sinking…and a debris field no more than thirty meters wide, with very little burning debris at all. But she was looking down at a debris field approximately two hundred meters in circumference and a burning oil slick where the boat should have been. There were large and small chunks of the boat floating on the surface on fire. The boat had been blown to splinters – disintegrated. The engines probably sank straight to the bottom, where they sat obscured from view by the burning oil slick. In the water in this location, which charts showed was about ten feet deep, she could pick out several large chunks of the boat laying on the bottom more than fifty meters from the estimated location of the boat when it blew. The Chief was right. This was no accident. President Russell' boat was blown up with powerful explosives.

There were only a handful of other boats in the vicinity. There was Captain Hal's tiny flats skiff, another runabout that was white with a red stripe and a red Bimini top closing on the wreck from about a mile away to the north. There was a navy blue with white trim and interior cigarette boat west of the wreck about five thousand meters with three people on board who appeared to be gawking at the site of the emergency through binoculars. A few more flats fishing boats were moving toward the spot of the explosion from various positions around the bay, most likely charter fishing boats with and without paying customers. In a couple more minutes, the wreck site was going to get pretty chaotic. Small boats from local law enforcement agencies had been dispatched to intercept those craft with the assistance of coordinates and descriptions from Lieutenant Biggers and her crew on board the HH-60 Coast Guard helicopter. Another helicopter from the Coast Guard station in Fort Myers was en route. They should arrive in about another five minutes. They were carrying an extra rescue diver. The Coast Guard had also re-directed a small patrol boat to the area, and it's ETA was fifteen minutes. The crew of that boat normally consists of three Coast Guardsmen under the supervision of a junior officer or senior NCO. They were lightly armed and carried considerable rescue gear for everything from Jellyfish stings to…well, this sort of thing. But what she saw below reminded her of the IED blast sites she'd seen in Afghanistan a few years back while flying medevac for the Army. Suddenly, she felt very inadequately prepared. She'd spent her entire adult life preparing for this sort of disaster, but now that she was here in the middle of it, she doubted whether the appropriate resources were in place. The Coast Guard had, of course, re-directed the nearest cutter and another rescue vessel that were patrolling in the Gulf of Mexico, but they were both hours away. How did Chief MacDonald end up in the middle of this? That was crazy! She knew of the former SEAL and genuine war hero from stories told by her brother, Sammy, when he was home on leave. She had never met any of Sammy's Teammates. When brothers and sisters both serve in the Armed Forces, times spent together are few and far between. Over the past decade of war, the operations tempo of the entire military simply didn't create many opportunities for family visits. When one was deployed, the other was in the States, and vice versa. Loved ones routinely passed each other like ships in the night. It had gone on for way too long, she suddenly caught herself thinking.

Interrupting a brief thought about her older brother, Sammy, the Lieutenant suddenly realized what she had not seen – something she should have seen. Where was President Russell' escort boat? Whenever a member of the Russell household went out on the water in their boat, a personal protection detail always tagged along in a smaller, faster boat. That boat should have been near the debris field, and those on board should be searching the wreckage. Should be – if everything were in order. But things were not in order. Someone had blown up the President's boat and the security patrol was nowhere to be seen. Sherrie decided to circle the helicopter back around close to the wreck at about one hundred fifty feet. Perhaps she had missed the small boat in the smoke from the burning fuel. En route, she needed to update her control tower back in Fort Myers.

Standing on the bow of the flats skiff, Horace heard Captain Hal begin speaking to the man on the phone who identified himself as Secret Service.

"Horace says we're too busy trying to find the other passengers to talk to you right now. He said to tell you to get out here with everything you've got as fast as you can," the big fishing guide relayed before hanging up the phone.

"Captain, I've got another body in the water about one hundred yards out at ten o'clock off the bow," Horace said.

Between the flames and roiling black smoke, Horace had caught sight of another body floating in the water. Motion and the dark outline contrasted against the water's surface caught his eye. Then it was obscured by smoke, the acrid smell and taste of which now clung like tar to Horace's mouth and nose. Closer to the epicenter of the blast, the smell and residue of burning diesel was now much stronger, and it over-powered any smell of the plastic explosives residue.

# Chapter IV:  Danger Close

# "Fortune favors the prepared..." ~ Louis Pasteur

Semtex manufactured after 1991 contains a chemical tagging agent intended to make it easier for bomb-sniffing dogs and even highly trained people to detect prior to detonation.  The most common version of the tagging agent is a compound mixture of butane and toluene, both of which are flammable in gas form.  It is a highly reliable version of plastic explosive for electronic detonation and is waterproof.  So Navy SEALs are very familiar with the red bricks of deadly putty.  When Semtex blows, the butane-toluene tagging mixture is ignited and consumed by the extreme heat generated by the explosion, but traces of the toluene gas are often detectable for an hour or more in the vicinity of the detonation.  Sometimes, pieces of debris will even have traces of the tagging agent that are detectable by demolition experts for a day or more due to the unique odor of toluene exposed to heat.  In the sea breeze of Charlotte Harbor, confounded by the smell of burning diesel fuel on the water, the unique odor had been the first smell of the explosion to hit Horace's nostrils as they approached the blast zone.  Then came the smell of diesel fuel and even the disintegrated particles of the boat, fiberglass, plastics, adhesive resin compounds, and such.  But the odor of the toluene in gaseous form instantly propelled to the outer perimeter of the blast radius by the shockwave got there first.  That's how it always goes when you blow this stuff.  On the water of Charlotte Harbor, even the light sea breeze would quickly disperse the residue,  making it undetectable even for trained bomb dogs.

The presence of Semtex was a pretty strong indicator of the degree of sophistication of a bomber.  Everyone in the EOD and demolition world knows that.  It is the preferred explosive of the world's most sophisticated terrorists and assassins.  On the other hand, there are two varieties.  One is military-grade, and the other is made for blasting applications in construction and demolition work. To get a bomb on board a former President's boat and remain undetected by the security detail run by Secret Service, it would have to be small. To do the amount of damage that Horace was witnessing here, it had to have been very powerful. That led him to believe the bomb was made from the more powerful military-grade version of Semtex. That didn't bode well for who they were up against, because the purchase, storage, and distribution of Semtex since 2002 has been very strictly regulated. A person or group had to be very, very serious about getting their hands on the material, and their bomb-making sophistication had to be well developed in order to use it this effectively in a marine environment. Navy SEALs spent months of the most intense training with the best experts in the world to learn to use it properly. And there are no Navy SEALs of average intellect. They're all bright, well-disciplined, educated, and exceptional learners with a knack for self-education and improvisation.

Horace caught sight of the body in the water again. As Captain Hal pushed the nose of the boat through the smoke and debris, what appeared to be an adult male's head and shoulders appeared upright in the water about twenty yards off the bow, still at an angle off to the left. Just as Horace caught sight of him again, he disappeared below the surface. When people are drowning they don't exhibit the classic splashing and thrashing and screaming that you see on TV and in the movies. Instead, they most often appear quiet and calm. You could even characterize it as relaxed. If their head goes under the water, they will almost without fail reach a hand up over their head as they descend. It's an instinct to keep some part of the body above the water – in contact with the surface – similar to how rice grows as a rice field is flooded and the rice plant struggles to keep the tip of the plant exposed to air and sunlight.

Horace noticed that the person in the water didn't raise their arms. Something else was odd about this second glimpse of the person in the water, but he hadn't quite placed it when he saw a diver about to surface next to Captain Hal's boat, directly off the starboard side and about five yards away. Instinctively, Horace flattened himself out on the exposed casting deck, releasing the lines in both hands. That's when he heard the sharp thud against the port side hull of the flats boat and felt a slight vibration in the deck from the impact. Intuitively, he knew that someone in the water behind him had just attached a contact mine to the boat – a task he had rehearsed himself dozens of times. The diver, wearing a black mask over wet black hair and a closely cut beard, emerged head and shoulders out of the water and lifted his left arm clear of the water. In his left hand, he held a Czech Scorpion sub-machine gun. The Scorpion is a pistol-like, fully automatic 9mm weapon with an exceptionally high cyclic rate of fire that is known for its dependability. It is favored for close quarters combat by terrorists from Eastern Europe, the Baltic region, and in parts of Asia. Rolling quickly into the main cockpit of Hal's flats boat, Horace heard the staccato reports of a burst of fire from the Scorpion. He felt the boat shudder, followed by a heavy thud against the gunwale on the port side that pitched the boat sharply to port. Glancing quickly to the console, there was no sign of Captain Hal.

The second burst from the sub-machine gun belched a volley of 9mm Parabellum slugs into the gunwale on the starboard side. Chunks of fiberglass ripped through the air over Horace's head. Reaching up onto the seat in front of the console with his left hand, he grabbed the tackle bag he had left there and pulled it to the deck. The third volley of fire from the Scorpion tore through the console above the seat, splintering the Plexiglas windshield. As Horace ripped open the tackle bag and retrieved his Glock 26 and two spare magazines, he caught a glimpse of something out of the corner of his left eye that he would never forget. One of the 9mm slugs from the attacker's sub-machine gun had scored a direct bullseye on Captain Hal's decal of the seal of the United States Marine Corps on the windshield of his boat. It's strange how things like that stick in your mind. Equally bizarre, this split-second sight is what triggered the first feeling of anger in Horace since this incident began. Trained to "turn off" their emotions like a light switch, SEALs rarely register and recall emotions during a firefight. Hopefully, the many months of rehab and civilian life had not dulled his fighting edge. He was going to need it if he wanted to survive this mess! Hugging the deck below the gunwale, the warrior stripped off the life jacket.

Horace knew he had to take his chances with the diver he expected to find in the water on the opposite side of the boat from where he was taking fire. Having just attached a contact mine to the hull...if his instincts were correct...that bad guy would not have a weapon at the ready, and would probably be swimming away from the boat. The mine would likely kill or incapacitate anyone close to the boat when it exploded, and you don't deploy them unless you intend to use them. Once in the water, Horace could use the boat as cover and concealment. His odds of surviving the attack of the machine gun wielding diver in front of him would drastically improve – unless the other asshole detonated the bomb. Horace would have to neutralize the gunman and put some space between himself and the flats skiff before that happened. He dared not think about Hal just yet. You can't help someone else if you're dead, but he feared the worst had already befallen his new friend.

Another short burst of 9mm slugs raked the hull of Hal's boat too close to Horace's head for comfort and he felt the vibration of slugs impacting too close to his body, tearing up the boat's fiberglass hull. It's go time!

Quickly estimating the point of origin of the gunfire by calculating the spot where he saw the gun-toting frogman surface, the reports from the Scorpion sub-machine gun, and the angles of impact of the slugs on the boat, Horace rolled onto his side, tossed the life jacket into the air toward the bow, and raised the Glock above the gunwale. He fired three rapid shots in the direction of his imagined target, visualizing the scenario in his mind. Immediately, he whirled his body and sprung from the deck of the skiff, propelling himself over the opposite gunwale with his legs. Using his left arm the way a gymnast does to gain clearance on the vault, he cleared the gunwale and splashed heavily into the sea. There was no time to search for the mine he expected was affixed to hull and armed to explode. He had to get away from the boat. Underwater, a SEAL has an advantage in close quarters combat. This was their specialty. Looking up, Horace scanned the surface from below, quickly mapping the burning oil slick, noting a couple of large chunks of debris, and orienting everything to the hull of Captain Hal's boat. The last time Horace had done anything similar to this, he had been able to stay submerged for over five minutes on a single breath of air, but he anticipated that his deteriorated physical condition would shorten that timeframe – to what he did not know. To be conservative, he estimated three minutes. Using the burning fuel on the surface and Hal's boat for concealment, he chose a course and began to swim – fast and straight, hoping to put as much distance between himself and the danger zone as possible. If he were lucky, he would also be swimming in a different direction than the second diver. If he was really lucky, there wouldn't be any more of these assholes down here! If not, he'd have to fight his way to safety.

Safety. What exactly was that, anyway? No one could have anticipated such a brazen, well-coordinated, and highly financed and equipped attack on a former U.S. President would occur in Boca Grande, Florida. This was insanity! But Horace had seen, heard, touched, and smelled more than enough of this sort of insanity over the past twenty years. While he wasn't expecting it, he was too well-informed and well-trained not to be prepared for it –
anytime…anywhere. The world is populated by more than its fair share of human predators! Sharks aren't the only dangerous creatures in the sea around Boca Grande.

"Shit. No time to think about sharks right now," Horace mused to himself as he swam for his life. The Glock in his right fist forced him to swim using a butterfly kick, not unlike the way dolphins propel themselves forward in the water. With swim fins on his feet he would be three times faster, but all of that great SEAL equipment wasn't worth thinking about now! As he swam, he was counting off the seconds in his head.

Moving to the East, Horace was swimming toward an undeveloped, wooded stretch of shoreline that began just South of downtown Punta Gorda. On the South end of this wilderness preserve, there was a marina he recalled from his map studies. The name wasn't important enough to recall at the moment. Several hundred yards off the shore, he would come to a shallow flat. Between there and the tree-lined bank he would be exposed to aerial observation. Hopefully, if anyone saw him it would be the good guys; maybe even Sammy's kid sister in her

Coast Guard helicopter. But Horace knew she already had her hands full by now – even if no one was aware that he and Hal had been attacked by highly trained, well-equipped frogmen in the debris field.

At the eighty-five second mark, Horace felt the shockwave of the explosion. A half-second behind the change in water pressure that popped his inner ears, he heard a quick, deep "thump." Without looking back, he assumed the second attacker had detonated the charge he attached to Hal's boat.

"God, I hope Hal's OK," Horace thought. Then the image of the bullet ripping through Hal's USMC logo on the windshield flashed in his mind's eye.

*No One Left Behind!*

The Navy SEAL mantra ripped through his consciousness like a serrated blade on a divers' knife. What was he doing? Hal was a Marine. "Once a Marine, always a Marine." Right?

"What the Hell am I doing?" Horace thought to himself while still swimming away from the scene of the attack. "I can't leave Hal out here by himself. Dead or alive, he deserves better. Fuck!"

A pang of guilt and disappointment pierced Horace's soul as he turned back to face his attackers in the dark, fiery waters. He paused to conduct a 360 degree security sweep of his immediate surroundings. He felt the first signs of oxygen deprivation. He had only been underwater for a hundred seconds.

"Crap, Horace, you're way too out of shape for this shit!" he chastised himself as he made a mental note that three minutes would be the maximum time that he could expect to say submerged on a single breath. His leg ached intensely, but he hadn't noticed it until now.

Approximately six feet underwater, Horace performed a quick self-assessment of his body, noting he didn't seem to be wounded and all body parts were functioning. Except for some abrasions he could feel due to the sting of the salty water, he seemed fine. Barefoot, he tucked the pistol into his trousers long enough to remove his shirt. Then he palmed the Glock 9mm handgun once again and double-checked the presence of both extra magazines in his pants pockets. He also recalled during this pat down that he had a Leatherman multi-tool on his belt and his Samsung Galaxy Rugby smartphone was still in his pocket, probably no longer functioning in spite of being able to withstand several minutes of submersion to a depth of about ten feet. He made a mental note to give it a try when he surfaced.

With less than a minute before the oxygen deprivation became a serious issue, Horace had to formulate a quick plan for trying to rescue Captain Hal. He knew all too well that he could no longer rely upon either the handgun or the smartphone. He couldn't imagine the multi-tool coming in handy as a weapon, but it could prove useful in other ways. He was completely without first aid supplies in the event of a major injury. So he tied his shirt to a belt loop on his trousers, thinking, "Not much, but better than nothing."

The saltwater was warm and comforting against his skin. He estimated the water temperature to be near eighty degrees. At least he didn't have to worry about hypothermia! Ball-parking his speed and elapsed time, he figured he was roughly two hundred fifty to two hundred eighty meters from where Captain Hal's boat was when he left. He had to assume the explosion he had just experienced was Captain Hal's boat, and that it was now scattered in tiny fragments all over the water and littering the ocean floor. The water depth in this area ranged from six to twenty feet. How deep it was at that spot he did not know. It was time to surface and take a better look around. He could re-oxygenate his body while he surveyed the surface. If he was lucky, there wouldn't be too much smoke, fire, or debris obscuring his line-of-sight. This situation was pretty damned ugly, but he'd been in worse scrapes and came out with all of his fingers and toes. There is simply no substitute for bold, quick, and unexpected action in the face of eminent death! It's far better to do something than to do nothing, even if you do the second or third smartest thing you can do. Indecision and inactivity get people killed. You can adapt on the move, adjusting your plan and tactics to match the situation as it unfolds. But Horace knew all too well that he had to do something these assholes weren't expecting.

One thing they probably weren't expecting was that a former Tier One Special Operator just happened to be fishing nearby when they attacked the ex-President. Figure the odds of that happening. Their plan of attack would have accounted for President Russell's security detail, but not for highly trained and well-disciplined bystanders jumping square in the middle of their little death party. Horace was the proverbial fly in the ointment, and he could use that to his advantage if he acted boldly and quickly. But he would need some luck and any and all help he could find. His new friend with the Scorpion sub-machine gun would likely be running low on ammunition, judging from the number of 9mm slugs he had pumped into Hal's boat. Any firearms these jackals were carrying were strictly for "last resort" types of contingencies. So they wouldn't be carrying more than one or two extra magazines. Horace knew he had already reloaded that room broom once. He also knew his adversaries were very skilled with explosives, and likely carrying at least one more small demolition device to deal with "clean-up" operations.

The other thing Horace damned-sure knew was that these guys he was facing didn't intend to get caught. They had to have an escape vehicle and pre-planned route. Judging from his first encounter, he could tell they were well-trained and well-equipped. These weren't just a couple of self-radicalized terrorists who dropped out of college to pursue their warped brand of Jihad. No sir! These guys were top notch assassins who were used to working as a unit, not unlike his brothers-in-arms from the Navy Special Warfare Command.

No one could expect to escape such an attack against a high-profile, defended target on the water within a mile of the U. S. coast by zipping away in a boat. That left only one real option, an option that only someone like Horace would be likely to consider: a high-speed underwater vehicle. The SEALs called them SDV's, SEAL Delivery Vehicles. SEALs had the best in the world and used them extensively to clandestinely carry operators further and faster than they could swim. Virtually undetectable from the surface, SDV's radically extended the range of SEAL teams, and were mostly used in intelligence gathering and salvage missions. They rarely used them in attack mode, because the vehicles were not defendable and would most likely have to be left behind once the shooting started. But they worked great for clandestine insertion for sabotage missions. A small group of SEALs could ride the submersibles like underwater sleds from far out to sea, carrying large amounts of demolitions munitions, dismount the vehicle near their target to place their charges, and then return to vehicle to facilitate their egress – all with a dramatically reduced risk of being discovered. Horace guessed these two (hopefully it was only two) clean-up men would be using a vehicle similar to this, but of a commercially available variety. Perhaps it was even manufactured by the team specifically for this purpose. In any event, there would likely be an additional "driver" guarding the sled not far from the area of the attack. So he was counting on at least three bad guys operating from at least one of what civilians called a "dive scooter," or DPV – a Diver Propulsion Vehicle.

---

Hal White maneuvered the small boat carefully along the line of bearing Horace had given him, scanning the water to his left for any sign of the body the younger man said he'd seen in the water. His eyes were stinging from the exposure to the smoke all around them.

Suddenly, the torso of a man Hal instantly recognized as a SCUBA diver emerged about fifteen feet off the left side of his boat. "What the heck was a SCUBA diver doing out here?" the older man thought to himself as he instinctively moved the throttle into neutral gear. In his peripheral vision, he saw Horace suddenly flatten himself out on the casting deck as he watched the stranger in the water raise one arm out of the water. He had something in his hand. Hal stared in disbelief as the recognition gripped him that the guy was pointing a gun at his boat! Just as he reached for the throttle, the diver trained the gun in Hal's direction. He felt the impact of the first bullet smash into the console of his boat. Then something hit him in the left side of his head above his ear harder than he had ever been hit before. He lost consciousness as he became aware of his knees buckling and his vision turning bright red.

---

Overhead in the helicopter, Lieutenant Sherrie Biggers completed her descent to one hundred fifty feet above the sea, and had turned the nose of the HH-60 Jayhawk toward the center of the debris pattern. Between whirling clouds of black smoke, she caught a glimpse of Captain Hal's fishing boat below and to her left at approximately fifteen hundred meters. Using the boat as a point of reference to begin a close grid search, she radioed back to Fort Myers that she was taking her bird in for a closer look at the scene to assist in the search for survivors. As soon as she finished talking, she saw Chief MacDonald fall flat against the forward deck of the small boat. She noticed movement on the water near the boat on the opposite side from her chopper. Then she saw Captain Hal White fall behind the center console, landing hard and limp against the near-side gunwale of his boat. Instantly, she knew something had gone terribly wrong!

Pitching the nose of the big helicopter forward, she added thrust and began closing the distance between herself and the fisherman's boat. She had to do a quick visual scan of the area, but her attention was now focused on Chief MacDonald and Captain Hal. As a wisp of black smoke cleared from between her chopper and the boat below, she made out the upper torso of a man in the water on the opposite side of Hal's boat from where she was. He was firing a weapon!

"What the fuck?" she shouted at no one in particular.

Her radio crackled in both ears with interference, probably from multiple people asking her to explain her excitement all at once.

"Coast Guard Fort Myers this is Candy Two Seven. I've got armed men in the water attacking civilians in the debris field. Do you copy? I repeat. I've got armed men in the water attacking civilians who are trying to render aid." Swallowing hard, she continued, "Get everybody you can to my location now, dammit! Right fucking now!"

Lieutenant Biggers heard her crew chief in her right ear, "LT – what the Hell is going on down there?"

Her right ear buzzed with the voice of Commander Johnson, "Candy Two Seven, what is your status? This is Fort Myers Control, over."

She moved the helicopter closer. Six hundred meters and closing at a surface speed of eleven knots.

"Control, this is Candy Two Seven. I have armed assailants in the debris field shooting people who were trying to help! Get the locals, the National Guard… Jeezus, get anybody with guns out here immediately! …over!" she screamed into her radio. The combat veteran pilot could barely believe what she was saying.

From two hundred meters, the Coast Guard Lieutenant saw Captain Hal was down and not moving, blood was everywhere across the stern of his boat…Hal's blood. She saw Chief MacDonald roll into the lower main cockpit of the boat and he was moving around. The gunman in the water, whom she could now tell was wearing SCUBA gear, raked the boat repeatedly with automatic weapons fire from a firearm he held in one hand. Amid spraying pieces of Hal's fiberglass boat, it dawned on her that the man in the water was firing some sort of small machine gun.

"For Myers Control this is Candy Two Seven. I've got automatic weapons fire. I say again, I am observing automatic weapons fire!"

"Holy shit, LT!" crackled the voice of her crew chief in her right ear.

"Candy Two Seven, this is Control. Abort. Abort your mission. Get out of there right now, Sherrie! Do you copy?" bellowed the voice of Commander Johnson in her left ear.

---

The Lee County Sheriff's Department water patrol unit had just pulled out of Gasparilla Marina when their radio crackled and the voice of the 9-1-1 dispatcher assigned to the Regional Joint Law Enforcement Marine Task Force broke the air.

"Lee County Water, Lee County Water, this is Tango Foxtrot One. Do you copy?"

Deputy Mike Simmons picked up the handset, keyed the mic, and replied, "Go ahead, Tango Foxtrot One. This is Lee County Water, over."

"Lee County One, there's been a report of an explosion on board a boat near Marker 19 over in the harbor. We need you to respond, over."

"Roger. Shipboard explosion. Vicinity of Marker 19. We copy and are en route. Can you forward precise coordinates, over?" responded the deputy.

"Roger that, Lee County Water. We'll give you everything we've got en route. Maintain radio contact on this channel for now, over," answered the dispatcher.

"Roger Wilco, Tango Foxtrot One. We are heading that way now from Gasparilla Marina. ETA is fifteen minutes," the deputy said before hanging up the handset. He hit the lights and siren, checked the channel ahead to be sure it was clear, and leaned into the throttle on the patrol boat.

---

By the time Horace and Captain Hal had headed into the debris field from the original explosion for the first time, the Regional Joint Law Enforcement Marine Task Force that serves the greater Boca Grand area was buzzing with activity. The task force consists of the Florida Wildlife Commission's Enforcement Division assets assigned to the area, both the Sarasota and Lee County Sheriff's Department water patrol units, and the local police and fire departments from more than a dozen communities between Lemon Bay and Fort Myers. Each of these participating organizations had airborne and/or waterborne assets that the task force coordinated for more effective emergency responses to incidents on the vast network of canals, bays, marshes, and islands in the area of Charlotte Harbor, Boca Grande Pass, Gasparilla Island, and Pine Island…as well as the numerous smaller named barrier islands and keys along this stretch of the Gulf Coast of Florida. The various organizations assigned to the task force trained and worked together daily, and operations were coordinated through the area 9-1-1 Emergency Response Center. They coordinated their work closely with the United States Coast Guard out of Fort Myers, but were a separate entity. In the event of a major incident, which was anything requiring state-level or national emergency response activity, then they quickly transitioned to the operational control of the Florida Department of Homeland Security. If there were ever an emergency of national significance, then operational control would transfer to the United States Department of Homeland Security. That local office just so happened to be a part of the U.S. Coast Guard station in Fort Myers. Everyone assigned to the task force had been subjected to drill after drill, covering every permutation of what sort of incident they were responding to and who had operational jurisdiction. Everybody knew each other. The game wardens from the FWC hosted a monthly cookout on the beach for all of the fire department and sheriff's deputies. They were all on a first name basis and knew each other's kids and spouses. The intimacy with the Coast Guard personnel wasn't as strong, but they worked well together. Personnel with the Coast Guard tended to turn over too rapidly to develop the kinds of long-term friendships and familiarity that comes from working side-by-side with local law enforcement or fire and rescue employees. But the Coast Guard folks were consummate professionals. From the eighteen and nineteen year old new recruits all the way to the Regional Commander, the federal folks were the best in the business; and far more adroit at getting along with civilians than the military folks tend to be.

Fifteen minutes into this morning's incident, operational control had transferred twice. That was very unusual. A group of men in dark suits had walked in to the ops center ten minutes into the event. The 9-1-1 operators had never seen them before. They were Feds. After a brief closed-door discussion with the shift supervisor, the announcement was made that the ops center was escalating to a National DHS Protocol reserved for major terrorist incidents.

A 9-1-1 dispatcher who had been on the job for almost a decade asked if this was a drill. The ops center supervisor told her it was not a drill. The ops center got very quiet for about thirty seconds. Dispatchers and staff shot worried glances at one another. Then the ops center supervisor stepped to the center of the room with one of the G-men at his side.

"This is Special Agent in Charge Purcell, from the Department of the Treasury. He's assuming operational control of this center and the joint task force under National Security Directive 415. He answers directly to the Secretary of the Department of Homeland Security. Ladies and gentlemen, this is not a drill," proclaimed the supervisor.

"Thank you, Captain Brown. Ladies and gentlemen, I'll be brief. Everyone here has very important work to do. You don't need to be distracted from that right now. You only need to know the situation we are dealing with appears to be an act of terrorism against the United States of America, and until we learn differently from the facts out there, we will proceed on that assumption. Effective immediately, there are to be no…and I mean zero…communications from anyone who can hear my voice to anyone who is not directly involved in this operation. No contact with friends, family, off-duty personnel, or the press! Got it? I want to see heads nodding. Good. This is what you've been trained for people. Let's make it work," said the forty-something guy in a suit and tie who called himself Purcell.

---

In spite of her Coast Guard training, common sense, and the explicit orders of her superior, something snapped inside the soul of the young warrior piloting the bright orange and white helicopter. She nosed the big chopper down and added thrust, causing the noisy bird to drop to less than one hundred feet above the sea and increasing forward speed. From just above the carnage in the waters below, Sherrie Biggers thrust her unarmed helicopter into the fight. Army chopper pilot training and instincts took over as her Coast Guard uniform and markings moved to the back seat. The safety of her bird and its crew became secondary to supporting an American warrior "on the ground" in the midst of a firefight. She couldn't do much more than provide a brief distraction, but maybe that would be enough. More importantly, it was all she had. She was not about to leave a brother in the heat of a fight!

Aiming the big chopper directly at the bloody, bullet-riddled deck of light blue flats skiff, Sherrie rammed forward and downward until she was less than fifty feet off the deck. Just as she was about to lose sight of boat and the men below her, she jammed on the throttle and raised the nose of the awkward airborne machine. Rotor wash cracked in the air over Captain Hal's seventeen foot skiff as the helicopter heeled and began to gain altitude, but not before pushing a dent into the sea below, turning everything that wasn't tied down into an un-guided missile hurtling away from the point directly below the helicopter and frothing the saltwater into a misty spray.

As luck would have it, at that very instant Horace made his move. Firing three quick shots toward the gunman in the shallow water, the former SEAL warrior leapt over the opposite side of the boat – completely unaware of the brave and decisive actions going on overhead and behind him.

The gunman saw the unmistakable helicopter in the morning sunlight behind his target, but he kept his focus firmly on destroying his targets. By the color, he knew it was an American Coast Guard helicopter, and that it was unarmed – harmless. But just as he realized that the chopper was moving aggressively toward him and what that would likely cause, his consciousness registered a flash of motion from the boat. Actually, a muzzle flash.

"What the…," thought the attacker as a blow like that of a hammer struck him in the left shoulder and his Scorpion machine pistol dropped from an instantly numb arm into the murky water at his feet. He felt the weight of the weapon tug against the lanyard attached to his combat webbing suspenders, and he knew in an instant he was out of the game. Instinctively ducking below the surface for cover and concealment, the last things he heard were the cracking rotor blades of the helicopter as the sea around him erupted into a chaotic maelstrom of light, shadow, wind, and sound.

---

From the vibration alarm strapped to his wrist, the second frogman received his partner's VLF signal to detonate the charge he had attached to the small, light blue boat that had arrived first on the scene in the aftermath of the first explosion he had triggered. Without hesitation, he pressed three times on the waterproof ULF detonator switch in his hand as he hovered in the water alongside the two-man dive scooter that was to be his means of escape. From five hundred meters south of the the spot of the original attack, he felt the shockwave before any sound reached him. A sutle "thump" registered first against his entire body, causing his ears to pop, followed by the muffled report of the explosion.

This second mine was much smaller than the one with which he had destroyed the fishing boat carrying the former President of the United States. It was one of three he carried in a mesh bag attached to the side of the air tank on his back. They were for the "clean-up." Knowing that anyone nearby was likely to approach the wreckage of the President's boat, and that they may well recover one or more of the bodies that had been on board – or even that someone might survive the initial blast by some strange miracle – firearms, smaller explosives, and knives were the tools for making sure the job was done right. The team had to work quickly and expertly. A lot could go wrong. And they only had a few minutes before they anticipated the arrival of first responders. They had to withdraw at the first sight of law enforcement.

There was to be no engagement with first responders of any type other than random civilians.

The dark messenger of death would wait here for another four minutes for his partner to return. Then, alone or together, he would fire up the underwater scooter and slip away to their mothership, waiting just to the northeast of Smokehouse Bay near Pine Island. There was enough spare oxygen and batteries on the DPV, actually designed to service up to four divers, to get the two-man team that far, a transit they had rehearsed twice in just under three hours, navigating by compass. The bomber moved to retrieve the scooter's anchor, one hand sliding over the line between the rocket-shaped craft and the anchor lying on the bottom of the sea in eighteen feet of water as he descended.

---

Horace broke the water's surface, exhaling sharply, then taking a huge breath of air. Turning a quick 360 degrees while treading water, he checked his immediate surroundings and re-oxygenated his lungs, brain, and muscle tissues.

The smoke and sporadic lick of flame sharply contrast against the bright blue waters of the bay to his Southwest marked the spot of the wreckage right where he expected to find it. He couldn't see anything else but water melting into blue sky in any direction. Then he heard the rotor-wash of the helicopter off to his left, probably blocked from view by the glare of the mid-morning sun. He squinted and turned his head back and forth to change the angle of view in an attempt to pick out the motion of the Coast Guard chopper.

Horace's scan was interrupted. Convulsions and searing pain ripped up his leg and into his hips and lower back. Every muscle in his bad leg was suddenly contorted in a massive cramp and his head dipped under the water of a small wave. He dropped the Glock pistol instinctively and pushed himself back to the surface with his hands. His leg convulsed with three more spasms in rapid succession, taking his breath away with each raging surge of pain. Both his calf and hamstring muscles were fully engaged in cramps, distorting his leg and rendering it useful for kicking. The pain only let off a little bit.

Spitting water, Horace cursed into the air. Now it was all he could do to keep his head above water. Without use of his legs, he couldn't swim. He couldn't fight. He couldn't help Captain Hal.

Horace's brain immediately switched to survival mode. He realized that the shock, exertion, and lack of oxygen had taken a toll on the recently-repaired muscles and nerves in his leg. Trying to relax the rest of his body and will the cramps from his leg muscles, he struggled to keep his head above water with broad, back-and-forth sweeps of his arms across the surface of the water. Another wave caught him in the face and he felt the rage boiling up inside.

"LT, I've got a visual! In the water. Seven hundred meters to port. Looks like he's struggling, LT."

The voice belonged to Chris Jensen, the Rescue Swimmer aboard Lieutenant Sherrie Biggers' Coast Guard helicopter.

"Confirmed, LT," came the voice of her crew chief.

"I'm coming around," replied the chopper pilot.

Chris Jensen was a rarity in the Coast Guard, a female Rescue Swimmer. She had grown up in the California beach town of Redondo Beach, and became an Olympic Bronze Medalist swimmer at the age of sixteen. After a few years working as a lifeguard on the beaches of Los Angeles County, Chris had joined the Coast Guard to become a Rescue Swimmer. She graduated first in her class at the end of training and was posted to Florida, where she had been promoted quickly after a series of impressive rescues. Sherrie liked Chris a lot. The girl was fearless and amazingly competent. Moreover, she was funny and likeable. The young guys chased her around like flocks of sea gulls following a shrimp boat, but she never let it distract her or go to her head. Sherrie guessed she got used to all the attention at an early age. In spite of that whole "Baywatch" thing she had going on in spades, the Second Class Petty Officer was all business when in uniform. Sherrie was lucky to have her on board her helo. She was the best Rescue Swimmer in the district.

Chris admired Sherrie from the day they met in the pre-flight briefing room. She had been told her new pilot was a former Army chopper pilot named Lieutenant Biggers. That was all she knew when she walked into the briefing room and saw a woman with auburn hair and freckles leaning against the conference table in a pilot's flight suit sporting the parallel vertical bars of a Lieutenant. Lieutenant Biggers had been drinking from a Red Bull can, which she quickly put down on the table as Chris entered the room. Straightening up, the Lieutenant walked right toward her and smiled, a crinkle in her nose, and said, "Petty Officer Jensen, I'm your new pilot," as she extended her hand in greeting.

Six months had passed, and they had worked and played together almost daily since then. Chris taught Sherrie to paddle board and took her to some of her favorite restaurants. She introduced the Lieutenant to a few of the guys she knew in town whom she liked, but were too old to be her "type." They were much closer to the LT's age. They went spear-fishing and SCUBA diving together in the Keys. The Lieutenant was dead-serious about her work. You always knew she was in command and in control. But off duty, they had become friends easily and quickly. Chris was grateful that the Coast Guard's policies about supervisor-subordinate off-duty relationships weren't as strict as they are in the Army, Navy, and Marine Corps.

"I'll circle around and take a look at the situation, but get ready to jump, Chris," instructed the Lieutenant.

"Say the word, LT! I'm on go back here," replied the Petty Officer.

"Chief, take a good look around and make ready with the basket," Lieutenant Biggers said into the microphone as she began to bank the helicopter into a turn.

"Roger that, LT. We're good to go back here," responded the Crew Chief.

The radio crackled in her left ear as the voice of Commander Johnson blared, "Candy Two Seven. Candy Two Seven! This is Air Control Fort Myers. Come in, over!"

There was no sense answering right now. Sherrie decided she would answer her boss in a few minutes, and tell him what she had decided to do.

"Candy Two Seven, report your status, over!" shouted her boss back in Fort Myers.

Sherrie Biggers surveyed the blue waters of the bay below and in front of the helicopter. She couldn't pick anything out of the twinkling glint of sunlight cast about by the light chop. Her Crew Chief vectored her in to a spot thirty five feet above and twenty yards to the South of the man that he and Petty Officer Jensen were watching struggling to keep his head above water below.

"Appears to be a white male, LT. He's in distress. I need to get down there!" explained the Rescue Swimmer.

"Chris, can you tell me anything about what he looks like?" asked the pilot.

"He looks like a drowning fisherman, LT. Dammit, let me go!" shouted Petty Officer Jensen.

---

The chopper crew had executed flawlessy. They did this almost every day, so it's not like they didn't get plenty of practice. Good crews knew that each time was a new adventure. Things could go bad in a heartbeat, and you never knew what to expect.

"What is your name?" a man yelled in Horace's ear as soon as the basket stopped alongside the hovering chopper. He could barely hear, but he knew the drill. "Horace MacDonald," he yelled back as loudly as he could.

"Get them in, Chief," Sherrie Biggers screamed into the headset microphone as soon as she heard her Crew Chief say, "We've got him!"

The two Coast Guard rescue workers expertly maneuvered the basket into the center of the deck of the Jayhawk and began inspecting Horace for obvious damage without so much as a word to one another.

"We're clear, LT," the Crew Chief said into the radio.

Horace felt the helo begin to climb. His rescuers were a man, probably in his late twenties, and a younger woman in the wetsuit of a U.S. Coast Guard Rescue Swimmer. These two were real pros who seemed to be used to working together under pressure. They didn't even speak, each knowing what the other was doing and what they needed. They handed things back and forth with precision and speed.

"I'm okay! I'm fine," Horace said while raising his hands. Then his leg seized up again and he winced in pain, grabbing on to the sides of the rescue basket with both hands.

"Lay still, sir," said the man in the Coast Guard flight suit, "We're taking good care of you. You are safe."

With that, Horace just laid back and tried to relax. He wasn't in control here. And he was in the capable hands of the United States Coast Guard.

The doors on the chopper closed and the Crew Chief handed Horace a headset.

73

"Put this on so we can talk," he yelled into Horace's face. Horace did as he was told. Suddenly, the world became a whole lot quieter. He could hear a faint electronic hiss – white noise from the open internal channel of the helicopter crew. Otherwise, he could only feel the rhythmic vibration of the helo's engines and rotors. He flexed his jaw and his ears popped.

"Where are you hurt?" asked the Crew Chief.

"I don't think I am, Chief. My leg is just worn out. I have cramps and muscle spasms," explained Horace.

"Which leg?" asked the Chief.

"His left one, Chief," answered the young lady Rescue Swimmer with a bit of a smile directed toward Horace, "You better watch out for it, too. This guy kicks like a mule!"

"I got it. Left leg. Muscle spasms and cramping. I'll get right on that, Mr. MacDonald," he said with a sideways glance toward Petty Officer Jensen.

"I'm sorry about that, Petty Officer. Totally involuntary – I promise," Horace said, embarrassed by his own frailty.

"Don't mention it, sir. I'm just glad to have you aboard," Petty Officer Jensen replied.

"Chief, don't call him 'sir.' That's Chief Petty Officer Horace MacDonald of SEAL Team One you've got back there," interrupted Lieutenant Biggers from the pilot's chair. "Welcome aboard my bird, Chief! You okay back there?" she added.

"Roger that, Lieutenant. I'm fine now…thanks to y'all," replied Horace, willing his leg to be still as it tried once more to contort into a wet pretzel.

"Chief MacDonald, please don't be alarmed, but you are bleeding. I'm going to need to take a look and get that under control," interjected the Crew Chief.

"Nah, can't be more than a scratch, Chief," said Horace as he lifted his head to try and get a look at himself. He could barely move. They had him strapped down like a corpse on a gurney. Geez!

"I'm sure it's nothing serious, Chief. But I need to take a look and slow that bleeding down. You just relax," the Coast Guard air crew medic explained.

"Jensen, get my light and a blowout kit from behind you. Will ya?"

"Got it, Chief," Jensen replied.

Blowout kit is a phrase Navy SEALs are familiar with. That got Horace's attention. The blowout kit is a first aid kit specially tailored to stop blood loss from serious traumatic injuries – like gunshot wounds. This couldn't be good.

Horace thought to himself, "Damn. I checked myself over. I didn't get shot. Everything was working fine...but in the water I may have missed the blood...and with the adrenaline pumping...perhaps...aw Hell!"

The Crew Chief went to work on Horace's left upper thigh, just below his buttock.

"Looks like something knicked you up pretty good, Chief MacDonald, but I've got it under control. Just a flesh wound. We'll have you good as knew as soon as we get on the deck in Fort Myers. There'll be an ambulance on the landing pad."

"Thanks, Chief. I really appreciate it. You folks are top notch. I mean that," Horace replied. Honestly, he was still a bit shocked that he had been dragged out of the water by a girl half his age and probably a hundred pounds lighter than him. Times sure were changing! And, for Horace, it had taken a toll. Suddenly, he was just very damned glad to be alive...again. The old warrior closed his eyes and focused on the rhythmic vibrations of the helicopter's engines. He was safe. And there was nothing he could do right now but make things worse.

# Chapter V:  The Illusion of Security

**"Security is an illusion.  It is an idea, a thought that is created in the mind.  Safety is learning how to protect yourself from physical violence; security is staying at home all day."**
**~ Tola Seng**

The four Secret Service agents had been bobbing around in the Boston Whaler since dawn, patrolling a five hundred meter perimeter around the fishing boat of former President of the United States of America Scott Russell.  The Russells liked to fish.  Boca Grande was one of the President's favorite fishing destinations.  He loved to fish for the big Tarpon that frequented Boca Grande Pass, Charlotte Harbor, and the beaches along Gasparilla Island during the Summer months.

Each year since he left the White House, President Russell took up residence in Boca Grande at his brother's beach home in mid-June.  He fished at least twice each week until the middle of August.  It took a lot to pull him away from Boca Grande and the big silver fish he liked to catch by trolling lures or drifting live bait off the stern of his thirty-some-odd foot long Hatteras sport-fishing yacht, *The Yellow Rose*.  Twice, the former President had stayed until the end of September – in years when the fishing had been particularly good following Hurricanes which had forced breaks of several weeks each in his Tarpon fishing schedule.  The Secret Service security detail lived in a guest house located on the estate in the village of Boca Grande.  It was choice duty for agents of the Protective Service Detail of the Secret Service, especially for the ones who were single and liked the beach.

Special Agent Billy Kendricks loved to fish. He also enjoyed SCUBA diving, windsurfing, and girls in bikinis. Billy worked hard for three years to wiggle his way onto the annual Russell detail in Boca. A native of coastal Georgia, Kendricks had joined the Secret Service when he graduated from Georgia Tech with a bachelors degree in Accounting. At first, he thought he would work in the financial crimes portion of the Department of the Treasury. But his outstanding performance in the skills associated with the Protective Services Division...marksmanship, hand-to-hand combat, and surveillance...combined with certain personality traits had proven him better suited to this type of duty than his academic excellence in the field of accounting and finance. Along with the growing size of the protective details in recent years, the Treasury Department decided they needed Billy's services more in the Protective Services Division.

Kendricks took to protective work easily enough. Over time, he became an outstanding Special Agent in the division, destined for an eventual assignment with a high-level VIP detail for a President or former President. He was an "up-and-comer." Then he heard about the "plum" assignment in Florida from a buddy who pulled two years with President Russell in Florida. He heard there were two spots open for the assignment coming up in a few months. He applied for the assignment, but he was not selected. But he was sent to the White House instead. That was a big step up...a huge career-enhancement if he did a good job in Washington, D.C. Frankly, Billy hated almost every minute of working in the White House. A Southern boy through and through, Special Agent Kendricks didn't care for Washington or all of the intense scrutiny from the tightly-wound senior agents on the White House security staff. Most of all, he didn't care for the mix of personal lives, business, politics, and government that was so amazingly...disgustingly...intertwined in the nation's capital; especially at the apex of power – the White House. Billy often mused that the most powerful politician in the world shouldn't really work from a home office. The complex and ever-present web of conflicts of interests disturbed him deeply. Maybe that was the accountant side of him. Perhaps it was something deeper – something from his traditional, southern upbringing.

To distract himself from the moral dilemma and monotony of his daily routine in Washington that he seemed so inescapable during duty hours, Special Agent Kendricks took up a new hobby when he was off-duty. To avoid the displeasure of his all-too-tightly wound superiors, he set up an anonymous off-shore computer account from which he played on-line casino games. He also used the surreptitious account to play Call of Duty, a first-person shooter videogame that was truly state-of-the-art. He would transfer small amounts of money distributed from the trust fund his grandmother had left for him when she passed away into a Swiss bank account. From the Swiss bank account, he changed hard currency into virtual currency with an illicit "gray market" global bank that only handled trans-national monetary transactions via anonymous user accounts over the Internet. It was almost untraceable. It was equally as likely to escape detection from by the U.S. government counter-intelligence agencies that tracked the financial activities of Special Agents with the Department of Treasury.

Kendricks was bitten by the gambling bug while he was a college student at Georgia Tech. Along with some of his fellow accounting students, Billy spent his Spring Breaks in the casino resorts along the Gulf Coast in Mississippi and Louisiana playing various poker games and Black Jack. At first, it was all about "the odds," an exercise in advanced theories of probability and statistics. He developed a fondness for Dominic cigars and Kentucky Bourbon during the long nights he spent in the casinos gambling on the money from his regular disbursements from his modest trust fund. It was all harmless enough and completely legal. He put half of all of his trust fund money into a savings account, from which he would make meager investments in stocks and bonds and buy the few things a typical college student needed to survive. He gambled with the other half. No big deal.

Billy actually won almost as money as he lost when he gambled. Well, when he looked at the results over time. Sometimes you win, and sometimes you lose. He budgeted a specific amount of money for each trip to the casinos. When it was gone, he quit gambling. He had it under control. He really didn't understand why some people felt addicted to gambling. For him, it was just another recreational outlet – one that allowed him to exercise his mathematical mind at the same time he was do something frivolous. The irresponsibility associated with spending money this way combined with his tendency to win more than most folks did made him feel good. It relieved stress and made him feel "reckless" all at the same time. In his last two years of college, he had actually made seventeen thousand dollars more than he had lost. What could be wrong with that? Right?

Ten years later and three years into his secret adventure into on-line gaming, Special Agent Billy Kendricks felt quite a bit differently about the dangers of gambling. The owners of the virtual bank he used, the President and Chief Financial Officer of Cyber Solutions Services, Ltd., Mark Cordell and Samuel White, were indicted on charges of international money laundering. The FBI and Justice Department alleged that they had conspired to make millions of financial transactions on behalf of Latin American drug cartels and several known terrorist organizations' financial arms in Bahrain, Yemen, and Saudi Arabia. Billy saw the news almost immediately and recognized the name of the company that handled his virtual currency. He knew that the virtual bank had probably been under intense scrutiny from the Justice Department and FBI for more than a year. There was a distinct chance that they had looked at his account activity, but he knew of no way that they could trace it him. He was still pretty confident in the anonymity provided by his Swiss bank account, and the fact that Cyber Solutions accepted anonymous accounts linked only to an email address meant that there shouldn't be any flags waiving for federal investigators regarding his own account. The email address was not easily traceable to him either. Not without a warrant. And the very first thing that happens when a federal law enforcement agent or person with a sensitive security clearance gets caught up in some investigative drag net is that the person's Special Security Office is notified. When the SSO's get these notices, they almost immediately call the person in and question them about their activity and any relationship to the questionable people or organizations that are the subject of the investigation. There were no alarm bells going off. Billy had not been approached about anything. So it was pretty safe to assume that he was still below the radar. Nonetheless, he knew the risk of discovery had gone up significantly. He resolved to stop visiting the on-line casinos and switch his Call of Duty account to his primary email address. Then he deactivated the virtual currency account and walked away from the forty three thousand three hundred and twenty nine dollars and fifty one cents he had amassed in the account. In a single day, he had lost more money gambling than he had ever spent on anything in his life. But it was over – and he was safe.

Three weeks later a woman sat down next to Billy at a coffee shop he liked to visit in Washington. Billy was enjoying a cappuccino to celebrate his recent appointment and impending transfer to the Florida detail for former-President Russell. She was a good looking woman in her late twenties, about four or five years younger than himself, Billy thought. From her clothing and general appearance, Billy assumed she was likely to be a graduate student at Georgetown or George Washington University. She carried a small Kelty backpack like students often use to carry their books, laptop computers, and various odds and ends to and from classes. She was wearing a New York Yankees baseball cap, out of which sprung a dark brown, curly ponytail about eighteen inches long. She appeared to be of Hispanic heritage, but had pretty a pretty light complexion for a Latino. Perhaps she was from mixed parents or Spanish. She wore a Tommy Hilfiger long-sleeved shirt with the cuffs turned up two turns on her forearms over a gray school athletic club T-shirt – the kind you can buy at Old Navy or Hollister. She had on a pair of khaki cargo pants and sneakers. The young woman ordered a Latte, and Billy thought he could detect a bit of an accent underlying impeccable and polite use of the English language. He was right. She was a student. Probably an international student. Billy noticed that she was in pretty good shape, with ample breasts and a slight frame. He guessed her to be about five foot three or four. Just on a lark, he guessed her weight at one hundred ten pounds. He also noticed that she had a small mole on her right cheek, barely visible below her dark sunglasses. Then he noted that it was a big odd that she hadn't taken off her sunglasses when she entered the coffee shop and sat down. Maybe she liked the image. Maybe she was hung over or had irritated eyes due to some allergy. In that case, it would point to a heightened sensitivity to her appearance…not all that uncommon in women her age, but potentially revealing about her personality.

Billy Kendricks was a highly trained people-watcher. As a Special Agent with the Protective Service, that was one of his most important skills. In training, the young agents were drilled incessantly on attention to detail, body language, and all sorts of human behavior. They were also trained to recognize disguises and pick threats out of crowds instantly based on their appearance, mannerisms, and behavior in relationship to the group. Some things you just can't turn off and on like a light switch, and sizing people up within a split second was one of them. It had social advantages in addition to being a prerequisite for survival in his occupation.

Thanking the barrista for delivering her Latte, the young lady took a sip and sat it down. She picked up her blue backpack and extracted a cheap pen. Billy drew heavily on his cappuccino and pretended not to notice what she was doing seated next to him at the bar. The young woman began to write on the cocktail napkin in front of her. Billy thought what she did next was a big forward and certainly unusual in Billy's experience. He wasn't much of a ladies' man. He didn't stand out in a crowd and considered himself to be a very average looking fellow. But this good looking your woman whom he had never met slid the napkin directly in front of him, looked directly at him, and smiled without exposing her teeth. Then she looked away.

"You may want to read that, honey," she said into the air loud enough for only Billy to hear her.

Billy smiled and picked up the napkin, expecting to find a phone number or address. At first, the numbers didn't make sense, but they were vaguely familiar. After a second or two of trying to make sense of the clearly hand-written string of numbers, it dawned on him.

"Oh shit!" he thought to himself. The number on the napkin was his account number with Cyber Solutions Services' virtual bank!

"Excuse me, miss, but what the heck is this?" Billy tried to feign confusion.

Turning back to face him directly, the young lady leaned in just a bit and smiled as she said, "That is your Cyber Solutions account number, Special Agent Kendricks."

Billy's heart leapt into his throat! His mind was racing, but his training kicked in and he contained his emotions. Instinctively, he controlled his breathing as his situational awareness heightened and expanded. Outwardly, he tried not to let his sense of alarm show.

"How do you know who I am?" he asked with a forced smile.

"That's not important, Billy. But what I say next is very, very important to *you*," the woman said in a half-whisper. Billy could smell the milky coffee on her breath.

"My employers want to meet with you day after tomorrow. You must not tell anyone about our conversation and you must not miss this appointment. You will come alone, no cell phone, and no guns. They are watching you. They are watching your parents in Brunswick, Georgia. Any lack of compliance on your part will have unfortunate consequences for them, Billy. Do I make myself clear?"

"Yeah. Sure. But I still don't..." Billy began.

"Shut up and listen, sweetheart. I'm not interested in your life story or excuses," the woman hissed through smiling lips. "My boss will call you in an hour on your cell. The meeting location and time will be disclosed then. Do not screw around with these people, Billy. They will kill your parents and then they will kill you. Do you understand?"

"Sure."

"Good. That's my boy," and now the woman smiled enough to expose perfect teeth. "I like you, Billy. I don't want anyone to get hurt. I'm just an errand girl, you see. I have bills to pay and things to accomplish. So I do what I'm told and I don't ask questions. You should try that approach, too, Billy. This will go very smoothly for your parents if you do. I promise."

Billy said nothing. He just watched as the woman got up, gathered her things, and picked up her Latte; which Billy just noticed had been delivered in a to-go cup. Without ever glancing away from him, the strange woman smiled widely now as she said, "Ciao, Billy. Maybe I'll see you again soon." Then turned and walked out the door and down the block toward the left.

---

Billy Kendricks moved from Washington to Florida in April, where he joined the detail of the Secret Service assigned to protect former President Scott Russell and his family. But his "plum" assignment that he had worked for three years to secure had turned into his worst nightmare the split-second he met that strange young woman in the D.C. coffee shop. He couldn't believe how quickly his life had been turned inside out. Yet, here he was. He was trapped in a situation you only read about in spy novels and see in movies. He just wanted to catch white-collar criminals, and maybe some organized crime lords. How in the Hell did this happen? It all started with a little harmless on-line gaming. Nobody would believe him even if he did tell someone. But his handlers had proven beyond a shadow of a doubt that they were very capable of killing Billy's family – not just his parents, either! His whole family…everywhere. This was insane!

If Billy went to his superiors with the Secret Service and turned himself in, he would immediately trigger the systematic assassinations of everyone he cared about. He had no doubt about that. He also knew that his career would be over and he might end up in prison. That was if these assholes didn't kill him, too! But the most crippling part of the whole affair…the thing that truly kept him from turning himself in…was that he had no idea who they were, where they were, or how to track them down. He was trained to avoid this kind of mess and knew the procedure for handling something like this inside and out. But he felt powerless, trapped, and completely isolated. He decided that his best way to proceed was to act compliant and wait for his handlers to slip up somehow and expose themselves. Then he would act! Then we would blow the whistle, regardless of the consequences for himself. He

83

just had to find a way to save his family. He knew the Service would protect them if they could. But these folks were three steps ahead of the game, and they would get to most of his loved ones before the government could even respond to the threat. His fellow agents would arrive at his parents and siblings home to find them dead. These people were very good and extremely serious. At least all they wanted from him was information.

Since the early Spring day in the coffee shop in the nation's capital when Billy met that mysterious woman, his life had turned into a constant debate between turning himself in and going it alone until the time was right. Living in constant fear and stress, he knew that he would ultimately…eventually…have to do the right thing and go to his superiors in the Secret Service. But he couldn't screw up the timing and get his parents killed. He couldn't get anyone killed. He needed more information to take to his superiors. He had to find answers to some of the questions: who these people are, how quickly can they get to his family from the time they are tipped off, and who else in the Secret Service might be compromised. If he spoke to the wrong people, or if they spoke to the wrong people, Billy's family members would likely be butchered. His mind whirled with possible scenarios – drug cartels, terrorist groups, and other dangerous characters doing the bidding of some of the world's richest and most powerful people. Was the kingpin actually the President or CFO of Cyber Solutions, or was it someone whose accounts and illicit business activities were compromised in the DOJ investigation? More likely, it was the latter. The founders and leadership at Cyber Solutions were mostly geeks – computer nerds and high finance number crunchers. They just didn't seem the type to have the stomach for this sort of hardball. He decided it was most plausible that it was one of the drug cartels or Mideast terrorist organizations caught up in the investigation into Cyber Solutions money laundering case. He knew there were well-established links between the cartels and the Mideastern terrorists. He just needed something to go on. Anything!

Billy's controller never contacted him directly. That first phone contact, which came precisely one hour after the mysterious woman walked out of the coffee shop in D.C., was another woman. She had a distinct accent. European, but she also spoke excellent English.

"Billy Kendricks?"

"Yes," he answered.

"Thursday. Nine forty-five A.M. The Southwest corner of the front stairs of the Jefferson Memorial. Repeat it," was all she said.

Billy repeated, "Thursday at nine forty-five in the morning at the Southwest corner of the lower stairs of the Jefferson Memorial."

"Yes. There will be a small package on the steps left at that location just before you arrive. Do not approach within fifty yards of that spot until exactly nine forty-five. Approach the stairs on the opposite side and walk across the lower landing. Any deviation and you and your parents will die. Understand?"

"Yes, I understand," Billy said.

"Good. See you soon, Billy," and the connection was cut.

Billy was able to trace the number to a block of phone numbers used by AT&T for disposable cellular phones. It was a dead end. He had called in a favor with a friend from the Park Police to get that far. He dared not sound any alarm bells.

---

At 9:45 on Thursday morning, Billy Kendricks strode onto the North side of the walkway approaching the Jefferson Memorial. Tense and in a heightened sense of awareness, he walked toward the monument's first flight of steps. In the distance, he saw someone in dark clothing sitting on the top step of the lowest flight of stairs on the Southwest corner. A split-second later, the figure stood up and walked up the stairs, disappearing inside the memorial building before Billy had arrived at the landing of the bottom stairs. He stopped for a second,

85

scanning the area for any trace of surveillance, anyone who seemed out of place, desperate for either a clue as to the identity of his mysterious new acquaintances, or for a sign that he was being watched. He noticed nothing that seemed the least bit out of place. He walked across the flagstones to the Southwest corner of the landing. It was a chilly Spring day in the nation's capital. The sky was gray and cloudy. A breeze blew up the stairs of the Jefferson Memorial off of the Potomac River to the North. On the top step sat a thick manila envelope. A visitor to the memorial crossed in front of him, oblivious to his plight. Closing the final fifteen yards to the envelope, Billy noticed it had black lettering on it. Glancing quickly around, Billy closed the final steps to the envelope. Looking down, he read the writing. It said, "BILLY." He quickly scooped it off the flagstone and trotted down the stairs, tucking the envelope inside the partially opened front of his down-filled jacket. He had to be at work in a few hours.

---

The envelope contained copies of details of a sophisticated trace linking Billy to his Swiss bank account and to the Cyber Solutions virtual currency account. It contained his "secret" email address, complete with the IP addresses to his home computer and cell phone. Details about Billy's on-line gambling, his trust fund, and the first two pages of what appeared to be his SSO file with the Secret Service were also inside. What didn't make sense was a large number of significant transactions in and out of Billy's Cyber Solutions account with which he was totally unfamiliar. He had never done these things, and a quick tally revealed that the transfers in equaled the total of the mysterious transactions out. It appeared as if Billy, himself, had been laundering millions of dollars through his virtual currency account. He was being framed.

Also inside the manila envelope he had picked up on the steps of the Jefferson Memorial were a series of very disturbing photos and corresponding notes. Photos of Billy's mother, father, and two brothers, along with their own wives and children were annotated with addresses, phone numbers, schools his nieces and nephews attended, and detailed analysis of their daily routines. It was obvious that his entire family had been under detailed, close surveillance for at least a month. Some of the images appeared to be from the prior Summer, but Billy couldn't be certain. Perhaps they had been following his loved ones much longer. Either way, these people were sending Billy a very clear message: we can get them anytime, anywhere, on very short notice. Billy was familiar enough with the intimidation tactic. He'd learned all about it at the academy during his training to become a Treasury agent. He understood the threat for what it was, and knew that whomever was threatening him was serious, well-financed, and very good at this sort of thing. Nobody wasted this kind of resources on a bluff or a hoax!

The envelope also contained a bright pink notepad sized piece of paper. Written on that piece of paper in blue ink was a date and an address to his next dead drop – in Florida. Two weeks. Billy whispered a single word to himself, "Jesus."

Billy Kendricks stepped on to the dock alongside the Russell family's boats in the small marina in Boca Grande. A pair of divers were rinsing the saltwater off of their gear, having just completed their sweep of the docks and the Russell's boats. He knew both men, members of the team sent to Boca every year during the Summer months to protect the former President, his family, and guests. The three additional agents of the sweep team were standing at the opposite end of the dock, their task completed, watching the first moments of a new day dawning.

"Morning, Steve," Billy greeted the gregarious half of the diving duo.

"Hey there, Billy. Just another day in paradise," the Secret Service agent said as he sprayed fresh water on a pair of fins and a diver's mask in a basket at his feet.

"Don't y'all know it," replied Kendricks with a grin.

Special Agent Kendricks' crew members were already aboard the Boston Whaler, the boat used to shadow and patrol around Scott Russell's Hatteras fishing boat.

"Fishing boat, my ass, Billy thought as he walked past the Hatteras.
"That thing is a yacht! These people have more money than my entire
graduating class from Georgia Tech."

Glad to be back in the Deep South, Billy liked Boca Grande. It was an
extremely affluent small village made up of multi-million dollar homes
belonging to many of the world's wealthiest families. Unlike Florida's
other bastions of wealth, Boca wasn't plagued by Art Deco, Ferarris,
and conspicuous consumption. It was a tribute to Old Florida style and
gentle Southern charm. But the place was immaculate and well-heeled
to the max.

"A guy could get used to a place like this," Kendricks thought to
himself as he caught sight of the Boston Whaler and the other three
Secret Service agents he would be riding with today.

"Mornin' fellas!" Billy called cheerily to his co-workers, who each
returned his greeting in their own personal ways.

"What was the hold up, Kendricks?" asked Tom Miller, the agent in
charge of the detail. Even though all four were cross-trained to do
everyone's job, Miller almost always piloted the Boston Whaler on
these fishing excursions. He had grown up in Mussel Shoals, Alabama,
and was no stranger to the coastal lifestyle. The gang of agents detailed
to President Russell joked behind his back, calling him by a monicker
they had concocted to fit his personality. They called him Captain
Tom-tom, because he had an annoying habit of wrapping his hands in
cadence on any flat surface he could find, as if he was a bongo
drummer; and because he never relinquished control of the chase boat.
The detail had been working together all Summer. Three of the men
and one woman were "old-timers," having all been with President
Russell's White House security detail. The rest were newer to guarding
the Russells, but Kendricks and Bates were the "newbies." This was
their first season. As such, they were low men on the totem
pole…regardless of seniority or pay grade within the Treasury
Department.

"I left some gear in the bunkhouse," explained Kendricks, referring to
the guest house they used as both living quarters and an operations

center during this seasonal detail. "Just had to run back for it and hit the boys room."

"Well, climb on board and settle in. Russell will be showing up any minute now. You know how he rolls," instructed Miller.

"Yessir, Captain!" quipped Kendricks to a snicker from one of the other agents as he climbed down into the Boston Whaler. Miller ignored the jibe and went about his business testing the radio on the control panel of the center console chase boat.

Kendricks and Miller were always on chase boat duty. The Senior Agent in Charge of the Russell detail had arranged it that way, citing the two men's familiarity with boats and fishing as his primary reason. The other two officers on the boat detail would rotate in and out every couple of weeks. There was an additional agent who always stayed close to the former President, whose name was Jones. He was one of the "old-timers" from Russell's days in the White House. Reginald Jones was a tall, muscular, African-American in his late forties who haled from Arkansas, where he had been a college track star who won a bronze medal in the Olympics and briefly held a couple of NCAA records. Russell was an avid runner and mountain biker, and Jones was one of the few agents who could keep up with the extremely fit former President.

The other two agents on the boat lately were Sandy Paul and Tim Smith. Both were younger agents than Kendricks, and Sandy was a young woman with an Ivy League pedigree who had been with Treasury only three years. She was a world class shooter, and the team's sharpshooter. She was also a former Olympic medalist, with two bronze and one silver medals in sport shooting events. A thoroughbred Yankee of Irish heritage from Rhode Island, she was a slight of build with fair skin, freckles, and strawberry blonde hair. Aloof and with a sharp tongue, Kendricks quickly decided she was too arrogant for his taste. He steered clear of her outside of work requirements. Tim Smith was a pretty typical guy in his late twenties from Des Moines, Iowa. He joined Treasury after a short but decorated career in the Army's 75th Ranger Regiment as a sniper. The kid had been awarded the Silver Star when he was twenty years old. He was all business and totally gung-ho.  The only thing outside of work that Kendricks knew about Smith was that he was a Star Trek fanatic, so he had been given the nickname, "Checkov," after the Russian character on the original Star Trek TV series.  But all in all, Secret Service agents were generally cut from the same non-descript cloth.  Lately, Kendricks had been feeling pretty out of place among his colleagues, like an off-colored patch sewn over a hole in a politician's security blanket.

"Russell's on board and ready to go.  Everybody set?" asked Miller.

"Let's go," replied Sandy.

"Ready," said Smith.

"Cast off the bow line, will you Kendricks?"  Miller shouted as he fired up the twin outboards of the Boston Whaler.

"Got it, Skipper," piped Kendricks as he leaned over the gunwale and released the figure eight style hitch knot in the rope.

"Let's go fishing, boys!" Sandy chimed in with a smile over the deep, guttural gurgles of the twin Mercury four stroke engines.

The Boston Whaler slipped away from the dock while as the dock crew was releasing the lines on Russell's Hatteras fishing boat.

"Keep eyes on, Smith," shouted Miller as he handed a pair of heavy binoculars to the agent from Iowa.

"Yessir.  Got it," replied Smith.

Sandy began to uncase her tactical rifle, a specially modified Heckler & Koch with a semi-automatic action, a custom weighted barrel, and ridiculously expensive optics and a composite stock specially milled to fit her perfectly.

Kendricks edged his way back to the center console, where he retrieved his duty bag and uncased an H&K MP5 9mm sub-machinegun with a harness that allowed him to carry it slung across his lower back and quickly swing it in to action should the need ever arise.  Per SOP, only the agents' sidearms, Sig Sauer P225s, were carried with rounds in the chamber. Kendricks nudged the slide lever on the sub-machinegun and looked inside the firing chamber. Clear. And he swung the weapon low over his right hip and donned a light windbreaker to cover it. The tiny marina of Boca Grande began to slip past the side of the Boston Whaler to the sound of seagulls rousted from their perches and a lone Great Blue Heron who was unpleased by the sudden activity this early Summer morning. The sun was just beginning to lighten the eastern sky.

Kendricks had not gotten any closer to unraveling the web he was caught in. Another note simply instructed him to include the days he would be off-duty for the next ten days on the back side, return the envelope to where he had found it, and leave the area immediately. The note said, "Do not look back until you are at least a quarter mile from this location or you will be killed by a sniper. Remember your family." So Billy did as he was told. Whether or not there was a sniper wasn't something he wanted to find out under his current circumstances. And that is how the communications proceeded: Billy scribbling down his days off on the back side of the notes in the envelopes at different drop locations in the vicinity of Boca Grande every ten days. These drops were in areas with fairly wide open spaces where the threat of a sniper watching him through a scope from some distance was very possible. Billy tried to tell himself that the information was relatively harmless, but he had been trained better than that. He understood that they were tracking his schedule in order to understand the comings and goings of President Russell – or someone else in his family. At any rate, he assumed Russell was the ultimate target.

Kendricks had started calling his parents several times a week to check on them. He kept the conversations short in order to avoid the temptation of tipping them off that something was wrong. Billy felt that the weight of the world was suffocating him. After another sleepless night, this morning he decided he had no choice but to turn everything he had over to the detail's SSO, John Jacobs, and take his chances. Yesterday and today were Jacobs' days off, and he always went home to Jacksonville to spend his days off with his wife and kids.

He had to set the wheels in motion in order to keep himself from chickening out. Before he went to the dock this morning, he decided to leave Jacobs a note requesting an appointment first thing tomorrow. The note read,

Mr. Jacobs,

I urgently need to meet with you as soon as you arrive. Please call me on my cell. I'll come to your office.

Respectfully,

Billy Kendricks

He stuffed the note in an envelope marked "Eyes Only. John Jacobs" and taped it to his office door. Then he grabbed his duty bag and the keys to one of their John Deere Gator ATVs and headed for the marina.

---

Miller kept the big engines on the Boston Whaler grumbling at idle speed as the four Secret Service agents proceeded out into Gasparilla Sound ahead of Scott Russell's Hatteras sport fishing boat. The radio crackled and Miller reached for the handset.

"Sparrow, this is Yellow Rose, over," the radio squawked.

"Go ahead, Yellow Rose, this is Sparrow, over," Miller replied.

Sparrow, Yellow Rose, we are underway. Everything kosher up there, over?" asked the former President's boat captain, Kyle Brenner, a Florida native in his fifties who had grown up in the small town of Placida, just across the causeway on the mainland from Gasparilla Island where the village of Boca Grande sits.

"Everything looks normal from here, Yellow Rose. Sparrow, out," Miller responded.

"Roger, Sparrow. Yellow Rose out," the radio crackled, then went silent.

The crew of agents on the Boston Whaler named Sparrow had passed the last No Wake Zone buoy outside the small marina. Now they were in the channel, and the crew was surveying the water in all directions in the dawn's early light. A couple of the same old commercial fishing boats were about, and there was a boat that looked to be a typical fishing charter coming down the channel about a half mile to their left. The horn at the causeway's drawbridge sounded. It all seemed like any other day on Gasparilla Sound. As Miller cranked the wheel on the Boston Whaler and put the engines in neutral to make room for Russell's Hatteras, a Manatee surfaced next to the boat and puffed a sloppy exhale into the early morning air. Kendricks almost startled. Smith chuckled and Sandy giggled just a bit.

"Wake up, Kendricks," she joked.

"Y'all caught that, huh?" asked Kendricks, a bit embarrassed. He shook his head and looked down at the deck. "Well, I can see what kind of day today is going to be."

---

On board the Yellow Rose, Kyle Brenner and his First Mate, David Crystal, had everything ready for a morning drifting live Menhaden and Blue Crabs off the stern of the Russell family fishing boat. Menhaden are a very prolific food source for all types of game and sport fish along most of the Eastern Seaboard of the United States and in the eastern Gulf of Mexico. An oily, silver-gray fish that averages about five inches in length, Menhaden…like Pilchards and Anchovies…make good Tarpon bait. What you choose depends on the time of year – on what bait fish are most common in the area at the time. In May and June, drowning chunks of Blue Crabs right in the passes was usually the most effective. As Summer progressed, Anchovies and Menhaden seemed to become the bigger Tarpon's favorite snacks.

David Crystal was a licensed pilot who had served as an infantry NCO in the 82$^{nd}$ Airborne Division during Desert Shield and Desert Storm. He had lost most of his hearing in a close encounter with one of Saddam's Republic Guards' artillery rounds and was medically discharged after the war. A native of coastal Maine, David decided to move to Florida while he was flying charter planes. But his hearing loss and a degenerating neurological condition had eventually caught up with him, and he failed his annual flight physical. He was grounded. That's when he took to fishing, a passion from his boyhood that now gave him both solace and a meager income.

Neither First Mate David Crystal nor Captain Kyle Brenner lived on the island. They lived on the mainland in Placida, a tiny hamlet which sat in the Southwest corner of Sarasota County and the Northwest corner of Lee County, where real estate prices and other costs of living were much more affordable than prices on the island. Most folks who work on the island don't live there. Instead, they commute to the island via the Gasparilla Island Causeway from Placida, Punta Gorda, and Englewood. People who live on Gasparilla Island don't have to work. If they do, it's because they want to.

"Good morning, Mr. President," Kyle said loudly enough to announce Scott Russell's arrival to his David, his First Mate.

"Good morning, Kyle. How are you this morning?" asked the former President of the United States.

"We're great today, sir. We're all ready to go catch a big one today. I've got some excellent bait and I'm taking you to one of our favorite spots this morning over along the eastern shore of the harbor. Should be a nice day today, sir," Kyle briefed the former President on his fishing plan.

"Captain Kyle, this is my niece, Shelly Lindsay," Scott Russell introduced a freckle-faced teenager girl whom Kyle had never met before. Behind her, the tall, African-American Secret Service agent who always shadowed the former President stood on the dock, his constant scrutiny disguised by a friendly smile.

"Good morning, ma'am. Welcome aboard the Yellow Rose," Kyle smiled and welcomed the youngster on board. Kyle liked fishing with kids. Whether it was catching Pin Fish off a dock with a six-year-old, or whether it was a teenager more excited about getting their driver's license or graduating from high school than they were about fishing, Kyle liked the less jaded and more innocent reactions of kids when they caught a fish.

"Will you be fishing with us today, young lady, or are you going along for a nice boat ride?" he asked.

"I fish, Captain Kyle. In fact, I've landed Marlin, Stripers, and Grouper, and I won a fishing tournament last year in Martha's Vineyard with a twenty-four pound Striper," the teen beamed as she laid out her bona fides for the captain.

"We've got our hands full with this one, Kyle," quipped the former politician-in-chief with a wide grin. "I promised Shelly we would help her land her first Tarpon while she's here this week. She's pretty excited."

"Well then we'll just have to make sure you get plenty of chances, young lady. Tarpon can be a bit uncooperative when it comes to actually landing them," Kyle said with a grin and a chuckle. He actually had little doubt that the teenager would indeed land her first Tarpon this week; if not today, then probably tomorrow.

"Well, I'm heading up to the cockpit. Y'all make yourselves at home. I'll send David to get you when it's time to fish," Kyle welcomed his guests aboard and turned back to the business of getting the Hatteras out into the harbor and finding the Silver Kings.

David cast off the lines as Kyle climbed into the captain's chair inside the cockpit above the main cabin of the Hatteras. Kyle eased on the throttle and the starboard diesel engine grumbled a bit louder in reply.

"David, grab us some coffee and come on up here for a bit," Kyle hollered down to his friend and deckhand.

95

"Roger that. I'll be right up. Try not to hit anything, OK?" David teased his friend as he disappeared inside the cabin to retrieve two cups of coffee from the galley and the big Secret Service Agent stepped on board the boat and turned to watch the dockside approaches.

---

As the Yellow Rose pulled out of the marina harbor on the back side of Gasparilla Island the Boston Whaler let her pass in the channel, taking up their position in the channel off the left side of her stern the better part of one hundred yards, but ahead of the wake from the Hatteras' twin diesel-powered propellers. Agent Miller knew that the captain of the Yellow Rose would begin to pick up speed now that he was out of the no wake zone and prepared to match his course and speed to the larger vessel for the duration of this morning's transit to their intended fishing area.

"Sparrow, this is Yellow Rose. We're ready to kick her up a notch or two and head across the harbor. Y'all good to go, over?" the voice of Kyle Brenner cracked over the encrypted VHF radios.

"Yellow Rose, this is Sparrow. We're with you, over." Miller replied nonchalantly.

The Yellow Rose began to pick up speed, and the wake from the boat's engines became visible. Kendricks felt the thick, Gulf air begin to whistle past his ears and buffet his cap just a bit as the bow of the Boston Whaler rose in response to more power to the twin outboards. After thirty seconds or so, Kendricks noticed something wasn't right. The Yellow Rose seemed to be moving faster than they were, putting distance between the two boats. He looked back over the center console toward Miller and saw the back of the agent's head. He had turned to look at the engines.

"We're not getting any power," Miller yelled above the noise toward Sandy and Smith. "Check the fuel lines, Smith."

Smith disappeared below the console, obscured from Kendricks' vision by Miller's body and the chunky center console of the Boston Whaler. Miller glanced a look of frustration and concern toward Kendricks before checking the gauges and fiddling with the throttle some more. Then Smith's head popped into view.

"Pressure's bad, Sir. Not enough suction. We've got a bad fuel line," he explained the results of inspection.

"Damn it to Hell," Miller muttered so only Kendricks could hear him. Then he picked up the microphone to hail Yellow Rose.

"Yellow Rose, this is Sparrow, over."

"Go ahead, Sparrow."

"Yellow Rose, we've got to stop and swap out a bad fuel line. Won't take long and we'll catch up. Everything looks good out here this morning, over," Miller explained to the captain of the Yellow Rose.

"Roger that, Sparrow. Informing principals now, over," answered Captain Kyle Brenner.

"Kendricks, grab the repair kit out of bow storage, will ya?" Miller said as he looked at Kendricks through the console windscreen and motioned with his head toward the bow of the boat.

"Sure," said Kendricks, moving forward to retrieve the kit, which contained tools and common spare parts. With outboard motors, fuel lines are usually the most common problem. So it was SOP to always have a spare on board the Boston Whaler in the repair kit along with spark plugs, assorted electrical components and connectors, a small patch kit, tape, and a variety of miscellaneous useful items like Super Glue, plumbers' putty, and a few extra navigation lights. Kendricks retrieved the box, dropped it on the deck, and opened it. No spare fuel hose.

"What the hell?" he asked no one in particular.

"What's up, Kendricks?" asked Miller.

"The spare – it's gone. There's no spare fuel line in here, Miller," Kendricks explained.

"It's got to be there, Kendricks. Come on, man. Don't horse around about something like this," Miller replied.

"I'm serious, Miller. It's not here. Everything else seems to be here, but there's no fuel line kit," Kendricks retorted over the sound of the struggling engines.

At that moment, the starboard engine died. Kendricks could tell from the reduction in noise and the fact that Miller immediately turned to look back at the motors again.

"Well I'll be damned," shouted Miller. Sandy and Smith looked concerned, but they had no idea what to do.

Then the port engine shuddered and fell silent. They were adrift. The Yellow Rose was pulling away.

Miller turned back to Kendricks and barked, "Bring me tape, putty, a knife, and the tool kit."

"Got 'em, boss," Kendricks replied, immediately setting about gathering the items Miller had asked for.

"Yellow Rose, this is Sparrow, over," Miller spoke into the microphone.

"Go ahead, Sparrow, this is Yellow Rose, over."

"This is going to take longer than I thought. Can you get Dark Horse on the radio for me, over?" Miller explained. He wanted to talk to Russell's personal body guard.

"Roger that, Sparrow. Wait one. This is Yellow Rose, over."

The wake of the Yellow Rose began to pitch the smaller Boston Whaler back and forth as the leading wave from the stern of the Hatteras fishing boat overtook the smaller chase boat.

"When was the last time you checked that kit?" Miller asked Kendricks.

"I haven't checked it in several days. When did you check it?" retorted Kendricks.

"Haven't touched it in weeks. I thought you were on top of it," Miller said as he stared back and forth between Kendricks and the shrinking stern of the Yellow Rose. "Dammit!" he spat.

"Better radio it in to the house," offered Kendricks as his mind began to race with *what if's*. He carried the load of needful things back beyond the console to the stern of the boat and sat them down on the bench seat.

"This isn't good," he said to Miller.

"No. No it's not good, buddy," Miller replied. "Y'all give us some room to work," he said to Sandy and Smith, who immediately jumped up and moved toward the bow of the boat.

"Sandy, take these and keep an eye on Yellow Rose," he said, handing the female agent a pair of powerful Swarofski binoculars.

Sandy took the binoculars as she stepped past the console into the bow of the Boston Whaler. She took up a position standing on the bow keeping a watchful eye on the Yellow Rose and her surroundings.

"Sparrow, this is Dark Horse. Come in, over?" came a deep voice over the radio speaker. Miller reached for the mic.

"Dark Horse, this is Sparrow. We need to give you a SITREP, over," Miller replied into the handset.

"Sparrow, this is Dark Horse. What is your situation, over?" the agent on board the Yellow Rose asked.

"Dark Horse, we are DIW – I repeat: DIW due to mechanical failure, over" explained Miller.

"Roger that, Sparrow, Dark Horse copies DIW.  Do you have an ETA for repairs, over?" asked the big man who guarded the former President.

"Don't know, Dark Horse.  It's more complicated that we thought.  It could take some time.  Y'all are on your own, over."

"Dark Horse copies, Sparrow.  I'll inform the principal and we'll decide how to proceed.  You gonna call it in to the house, over?" asked the elder agent.

"Roger, Dark Horse.  We're calling it in now and we will keep you informed.  This is Sparrow, over," Miller said as his shoulders slumped and he sighed out loud.

"Roger that, Sparrow.  This is Dark Horse, standing by, over," came the deep voice from the speaker.

"Geez, Kendricks.  You said it was gonna be one of those days, didn't you?"  Miller looked at Kendricks and faked a half-hearted smile.

"Yeah.  Yeah I did," said Kendricks, who suddenly found himself wishing he had taken action sooner.  He gazed off into the distance at the shrinking form of the Yellow Rose as she sailed off into the morning on the hunt for Tarpon.  He thought to himself, "I hope to God no one is hunting you, today."

# Chapter VI: SNAFU

## "No good deed goes unpunished." ~ Clare Boothe Luce

"Chief, we're about to land," the crew chief's voice in his ear snapped him back to full consciousness and Horace gave a quick thumbs up to acknowledge the message.

The crew chief and diver were strapping themselves in to their jump seats. All of the gear and packaging from dressing Horace's wound had been cleared away and secured.

The big helicopter banked into a wide turn as Lieutenant Sherrie Biggers surveyed the landing pad and its vicinity, making a final safety sweep prior to landing. Seconds later, the bird slowed and began to descend toward the tarmac below.

Horace's Teammate's kid sister sat the big chopper down on the deck gentle as a wind-blown feather lighting on the grass. The crew chief and diver unbuckled and began prepping Horace for deplaning and what he expected to be a quick trip to a waiting ambulance. While he didn't really think all that fuss was necessary, he knew that the Coast Guard had their SOP. He figured they would insist that he be taken to the hospital and checked out thoroughly. He knew it would be futile to resist, and he sure didn't want to give his rescuers any grief. So, for now, he decided to just go with the flow.

"Chief, would you rather walk? Do you feel up to it?" the helicopter crew chief asked via the headset as the blades of the chopper began to slow.

"Hell yeah, I'd rather walk," Horace said with a smile and a quick laugh. "Thanks for asking."

"Then let's get you unhooked," replied the crew chief.

A minute later, the young diver wrenched open the side door of the HH-60 Jayhawk to a blast of tropical air, superheated by the sun reflecting off the hot tarmac upon which the bird now sat. The blades had stopped and the engines shut down. It's always oddly peaceful inside a helicopter for the first minute or so after a landing when the engines are cut off. The contrast was particularly powerful today, after what Horace had just been through. A rush of names, call signs and faces of his former Teammates swept through his mind, followed by a wave of emotion. Horace missed his brothers back at the Teams. He suddenly felt very alone as he flexed his muscles to make sure everything was going to work properly when he stood up – another new habit he had developed since his big brush with destiny that ended his career.

The Second Class Petty Officer who had pulled Horace from the water deplaned first, took a quick look around, and turned back to face Horace inside the helicopter. The crew chief took Horace's headset and stowed it.

"After you, Chief," the smiling Coast Guard Chief Petty Officer said with a quick gesture toward the doorway.

Horace swung his legs to the steel deck of the bird and slowly stood up. His leg was weak and jittery. For the first time, he became aware of the numerous scrapes and small cuts on his back and arms, and he felt a twinge of pain and the pressure of the dressing on the wound high on the back of his left thigh. That frogman had almost shot him in the butt. Damn. Nodding to the young Petty Officer on the tarmac, who was now watching him intently, he grabbed the doorway with his right hand as he stepped down – good leg first – to the pavement below. Horace felt his left leg give way due to lack of strength and a quick shot of pain ripped through the nerves from his ankle to his hip. He didn't let on. Pausing just long enough to regain his composure, he lowered his injured leg to the helipad and stood upright, releasing his grip on the side of the helicopter. Petty Officer Jensen smiled.

Stepping away to clear the doorway for the Chief, Horace surveyed his surroundings. What he saw was unexpected. About thirty yards away from the helicopter on the tarmac stood a five-man security detail in full tactical gear. Each man had an unslung M4 assault rifle in his hands at the "low ready." Their faces were covered by hoods and goggles under tactical helmets of the variety worn by the US Army, but painted flat black. Just to the right of this little welcoming party stood two guys in gray suits and dark sunglasses, jackets open and exposing white shirts, dark ties, and semi-automatic handguns in belt holsters. There were badges on their breast pockets, but Horace couldn't make them out at this distance in the glaring sun. Lieutenant Biggers came around the nose of her helicopter, sweating, and strings of her long, red hair torn loose from her pin-up job as if she had torn her flight helmet off with abandon.

"Chief MacDonald," she said as she extended her hand in greeting. Horace exchanged firm handshakes with the pilot.

"Welcome to United States Coast Guard Station Fort Myers, Chief. Don't worry about those clowns. They're feds. They've taken over the whole damned place. My CO is pissed," the Lieutenant explained.

As the crew chief disembarked the helicopter, the two suits moved briskly forward. Their security detail moved, putting some distance between themselves and keeping clear lanes of fire between their bosses and the chopper. Horace thought, "Well, at least they seem to know what they're doing."

"I can't thank y'all enough, Lieutenant. You saved my ass back there. But before these clowns ruin the rest of our day, I need to know what you know about Hal…please," Horace replied to the Sherrie Biggers' brief SITREP.

"I'm sorry, Chief, but I won't bullshit you. Your friend didn't have a chance. We lost sight of him after his boat blew, but he was already down and in very bad shape. He took a head shot, Chief," the young woman's words trailed off at the end as she delivered the news Horace had feared and hoped that he wouldn't hear. But he had to know.

Horace broke eye contact with his former Teammate's kid sister and looked at his feet for a second. He swallowed hard and looked back into her eyes.

"Thank you, Sherrie. I had to know," he said.

"I know, Chief. I know...I'm so sorry."

"Horace MacDonald..." a voice interrupted their silent gaze. It was one of the suits.

"Are you Horace MacDonald?" asked the shorter, bald-headed member of the two-man team of suited feds now standing ten feet from Horace and his rescuers.

"Yessir. I am Horace MacDonald. Who are you?" replied Horace, turning to face the two feds. The one doing the talking was about 5'9" tall, a bit overweight, and probably in his late thirties. His head was shaved and darkly tanned. He wore a pair of Rayban Aviators with gold wire frames and dark gray lenses with a mirror coating, a calculated choice no doubt to increase his command presence by going "old school." His partner wore almost an identical suit and tie, but he was taller...about six feet...and more athletic. His hair was cropped close to the scalp and showed salt-n-pepper in the Florida sunlight. He wore a pair of black, wrap-around Wiley X glasses. Prior military. Probably Army. Both mean wore Treasury Agent badges on the breast pockets of their jackets. Considerable sweat stains showed on their shirts and beads of perspiration were noticeable on their foreheads. It was hot, but they had been under considerable stress for awhile, too. They were probably nervous. Both men carried Sig Sauer 9mm pistols, holstered securely at their belts and visible only when the sea breeze lifted their jacket away from their torsos. The silent member of the pair...the taller guy in the Army glasses...had a Mediterranean look about him: the dark hair, weathered olive complexion, and thick brows visible even behind the sunglasses. Horace noted that he was missing most of the pinky finger on his left hand.

"Mr. MacDonald, we're going to have to ask you to come with us, sir," explained the talkative one.

"I asked you who you are," replied Horace calmly.

"Sorry. I'm Special Agent Griggs and this is Special Agent Torres. We're from the Secret Service, sir. And we need you to come with us, please. Now…"

Lieutenant Biggers interrupted over Horace's left shoulder as she stepped up to his side, squaring off against the two feds, "Chief MacDonald (she said it with emphasis) needs medical attention, gentlemen. He's in my care until I release him to the doctors at the clinic."

"I'm sorry, Lieutenant, but you need to check with your superiors. I'm going to ask you not to impede our investigation again," snapped the chubby, bald Treasury Agent.

"That's enough," Horace said. "I don't know who you are or who sent you on whose authority. Show me some ID. But in the meantime, you'd be wise to adjust your attitude and remember your manners until we straighten this out, Special Agent Griggs. You'll get a lot more of whatever cooperation you seek without being disrespectful and trying to pull rank…which you don't have in my universe. You come out here without the station commander, armed to the teeth, and acting like you own the joint. Well this ain't my first rodeo, partner. And this young lady and her crew just saved my ass out there. You're just a stranger in a costume with a story. You feel me?"

"Again, I apologize for my abruptness," he said with a nod toward Lieutenant Biggers. "But, Chief MacDonald, you have no choice in this matter and I don't have time to dick around out here. You know the drill. My authority comes straight from the highest levels in DC. We're all on the same team here."

"Griggs, I don't have a team anymore," said Horace. "The only team I've belonged to since high school is up in Norfolk, Virginia. And I'm pretty damned sure you ain't never been in the Navy. It's been a rough day and…"

"Horace MacDonald, you are under arrest. Turn around and put your hands on your head," interrupted Special Agent Griggs in his most commanding voice.

Horace saw both agents' posture change as they shifted their balance, and Agent Torres (if that was really his name) reached to rest his right hand on the holstered pistol under his jacket. The five man tactical team behind the suits began to move. Horace saw the two outside men, designated overwatch, raise their rifles and point them in the general direction of the Coast Guard crew flanking him while the other three moved forward quickly, weapons at port arms. One quickly slung his rifle and reached into his vest – probably for handcuffs. He and the Coast Guard crew were completely exposed on the open tarmac of the helipad.

"What the fuck…" Sherrie Biggers exclaimed.

"Stand down, Leiutenant!" bellowed Special Agent Griggs. "All of you – stand the fuck down!" He was referring to the chopper crew.

The one called Torres unsnapped his holster.

"Stop it!" yelled Horace. "Everyone stop…and chill out."

"Horace MacDonald, you are under arrest on suspicion of conspiracy to assassinate President Russell. Now turn around and put your hands on your head. Don't let this get ugly!" Griggs snapped. The tension bordered on fear in his voice, and Horace knew that someone was going to get hurt unless he complied. He wasn't going to let that happen. He'd had enough for one day.

Just as the tactical team members flanked the two suits, Horace slowly raised his hands. Locking his fingers on top of his scalp, he slowly turned to face the helicopter door from which he had just emerged.

"Jesus Christ," muttered the Coast Guard Chief Petty Officer.

"This is wrong," said Petty Officer Jensen.

As the officer with the handcuffs stepped forward to cuff Horace, Lieutenant Biggers said, "You assholes are making a huge mistake. You have not heard the end of this."

The tactical officer grabbed Horace firmly by one wrist and wrenched his arm behind his back, quickly cuffing him with one bracelet of the handcuffs. He offered no resistance. Then the other hand was drawn down behind his back and locked into the second bracelet. The masked cop said, "Turn around," and placed his hand on Horace's elbow to indicate the direction he wanted him to turn, ready to control his movements if necessary. It wouldn't be. Not now. Not here, with innocent public servants in the way.

Horace heard a vehicle on the tarmac and assumed it would be a black Suburban. As he turned around to face agents Griggs, Torres, and their band of merry masked men, his suspicions were confirmed. There were two of them, to be precise. Four more suits piled out. Then everyone climbed into the vehicles and the whole entourage quickly whisked Horace away.

On the helipad, Lieutenant Biggers and her crew were left standing with their jaws on the deck and their heads spinning as the black Suburbans with federal license plates sped away.

Petty Officer Jensen asked, "What the fuck just happened, Lieutenant?"

"A major goddamned cluster fuck, Jensen. I'm proud of you two. You did a great job today. But this was a major goddamned cluster fuck. I'm gonna go inside and get to the bottom of this. And I've got to make a phone call to Virginia."